Gressingham

Gressingham

©2020 Gressingham Foods Ltd &
Meze Publishing Ltd. All rights reserved

First edition printed in 2020 in the UK

ISBN: 978-1-910863-68-8

Special thanks to: The Buchanan family and
Galton Blackiston

Written by: Katie Fisher

Edited by: Phil Turner, Rebecca Alderton

Designed by: Paul Cocker, Paul Stimpson and
Phil Turner

Recipes by: Vernon Blackmore (unless stated)

Photography by: Tim Green

Food styling: Katherine Connor

Additional photography:
Julia Holland / Galton Blackiston portrait

Contributors: Rebecca Alderton, Steve Curzon,
Michael Johnson, Tara Rose, Paul Stimpson,
Esme Taylor, Emma Thomas, Emma Toogood

Printed in Great Britain by Bell and Bain Ltd, Glasgow

me:ze
PUBLISHING

Published by Meze Publishing Limited
Unit 1b, 2 Kelham Square
Kelham Riverside
Sheffield S3 8SD
Web: www.mezepublishing.co.uk
Telephone: 0114 275 7709
Email: info@mezepublishing.co.uk

Foreword
Galton Blackiston

For me, quality and consistency are the most important things in cooking and that's exactly what you get with Gressingham.

I worked with their products for a long time, but even years ago before that relationship started, everybody knew of Gressingham. It's such a strong brand, especially in the Lake District where I was working at the time in the early stages of my career as a chef.

When I established Morston Hall on the beautiful North Norfolk coast, Gressingham asked whether I would try their duck in the restaurant. Anything of quality that still manages to be family-run, I'm more than happy to get involved with, and the fact that they're based in East Anglia was the cherry on top.

Since then, Morston Hall has held a Michelin Star for over 20 years, so I'd say we were a pretty good brand ambassador in return! Alongside being owner and chef patron of my country hotel, I started working in television and became somewhat known for the fact that my appearances usually involve me promoting seasonal and regional food.

I've always been someone who expanded slowly; projects don't interest me unless I can completely control their direction. In this sense, Gressingham products were a perfect fit for my ethos because they're so consistent. You can buy whole ducks, duck legs, duck breasts and get the same size time after time because there's such attention to detail in the way they raise the birds. That's evident even in the amount of fat on them; it's always a decent proportion - not huge layers like some consider the best - because actually rendering down lots of fat isn't that easy, and makes it harder for home cooks to get good results too.

Then there's the taste; I wouldn't have used Gressingham duck if it didn't have an excellent flavour. I've also used their guinea fowl before, and again the quality and consistency is what really impressed me.

It's true that I'm very biased towards East Anglia; you'll always hear me talking about what a brilliant area it is on Saturday Morning with James Martin, and because I'm from the county there's strong home ties too. Gressingham is a great example of the wonderful produce here; now in their fiftieth year, it's a brilliant thing they do by making duck so accessible to everyone.

Galton Blackiston

QUICK AND EASY DISHES

ASIAN DISHES

DATE NIGHT

DISHES FOR SHARING

REMARKABLE ROASTS

TRIMMINGS

DISHES FOR ENTERTAINING

SIMPLE SAUCES

This book marks a very special moment in time for Gressingham, celebrating 50 years of the family business founded by Maurice and Miriam Buchanan. Since its humble beginnings, Gressingham has become the foremost name for top quality duck in the UK, alongside hugely popular turkey and goose for Christmas and speciality poultry that makes any mealtime memorable. The company's excellent reputation and continued success is thanks to the passion, dedication and genuine care of the Buchanan family and all the farmers, suppliers and staff who contribute to every stage of production. From a trainload of ducklings to a high end brand recognised across the country, the story of Gressingham begins in 1971...

Having moved to England from Northern Ireland, Maurice and Miriam Buchanan established their farm in Debach, Suffolk with two sheds built by hand and a small flock of chickens. By the late 1980s they had expanded to own three farms, but then decided to try something a little different. The Gressingham founders got in contact with a small-scale duck farmer in the Lake District, Peter Dodd, who had begun to develop a cross breed between the popular Pekin duck and the Wild Mallard, which has more breast meat and a distinctive gamey flavour. In 1989, the first Gressingham Ducks arrived at the family farm in Debach; 500 ducklings were transported by train from Peterborough to Cambridge where they were picked up by Maurice and Miriam. Over the following two years, they perfected the breed and the remarkable Gressingham Duck, named after the village where Peter Dodd lived and worked, was born.

By this time, their son William had finished university – having studied agriculture, and written his dissertation on the development of Gressingham Duck – and was well placed to help his parents set up the new venture. A couple of years later, his brother Geoff joined the family business, and the two of them are still in charge of the farm today. "As a business, we wanted to be in control of our own destiny, make our own products, do our own sales and marketing," explains William. "The whole point is to create products that our customers enjoy; their support has always been, and continues to be, really important to us."

Throughout the early 1990s, Gressingham went through a process of transition from the initial 500 ducks a week to several thousand, as the Buchanan family gradually grew their production and found new markets by moving away from chicken farming. They started by knocking on restaurant doors, but soon built up a network of wholesalers to become well established in the food service industry, known for their quality and consistency. Although there were lots of competitors in the duck market, they were generally only producing whole ducks, and it wasn't a huge sector overall, particularly in retail. This was where Gressingham set itself apart.

Gressingham had created a niche to sidestep both these issues: their products were more accessible, easier to cook and more convenient for people to use at home as well as in restaurants. Offering precision-cut breast and leg portions was the first step to easy yet luxurious home cooking, followed by the Bistro range of restaurant-style dishes that met customers' desires for delicious meals ready in just 30 minutes. Now, anyone could enjoy duck without having to prepare and cook the whole bird, and thanks to its well-earned reputation as an upmarket brand Gressingham products were soon widely stocked in shops far beyond the Suffolk farms. Their first supermarket stockist was Sainsburys, who offered them a trial with two products across 20 shops, and are still their largest retail customer to date.

Part of the brand's broad and long-lasting appeal is the unique farming system, and of course the special Gressingham breed. The ducks are raised in buildings designed specifically for that purpose on the farms in East Anglia, which are all Red Tractor Assured. This means they are regularly, independently audited across a wide range of standards covering animal welfare, biosecurity, food safety, stockmanship and the environment. Health and welfare is an absolute priority for Gressingham, so all the birds benefit from natural ventilation, daily fresh straw and access to water for preening. The Buchanan family and those employed by them believe that this approach ensures the best possible outcome for their flocks.

It's not just ducks that are bred, hatched and reared on Gressingham farms; turkeys and geese are also produced for the festive season to the same high standards of quality. Both are very seasonal; the first goose eggs usually appear around Valentine's Day and the goslings hatch about a month later. The geese are then raised on open pasture in Norfolk for the remainder of the year. Turkeys are produced on farms across East Anglia where they range freely in grassy meadows.

William and Geoff have also partnered with the Léon family in Brittany, northwest France, who rear poussin and guinea fowl which are sold by Gressingham in the UK. Their poussin are the same breed as the country's top quality chicken, Label Rouge, which are slow-growing and raised in high welfare conditions, known for their flavour and environmentally friendly practices. Whoever they choose to work with, it's important to the company that suppliers, farmers and stockists recognise the values and qualities that have always set Gressingham products apart.

One generation and five decades on from its origins, the Gressingham brand is highly respected and known throughout the UK for its unique and delicious duck, as well as seasonal and speciality poultry that guarantees a luxurious, memorable meal, whether cooked at home or in a restaurant kitchen. As Maurice, Miriam, William and Geoff Buchanan celebrate the company's 50th anniversary, they are delighted to continue creating products that customers enjoy and to employ a host of fantastic people who help make this unique company what it is every day.

A Guide to Cooking with Duck and Speciality Poultry

By Vernon Blackmore, Recipe Consultant and Development Chef

I have worked with Gressingham as a recipe consultant and development chef for nearly 30 years now, and as a restaurateur their products have been a constant on my menus. The consistency, flavour and versatility of Gressingham duck products lends them to endless global flavours: think of classic Oriental crispy duck pancakes or the more traditional French duck à l'orange and confit. However, duck works just as well with pasta dishes, stir fries, Thai curries, on a barbecue and much more. I love marinades and subtle seasonings; Chinese five spice or paprika sprinkled over the skin are favourites of mine.

Cooking with duck can seem daunting at first, but once you have mastered a few simple cooking techniques, there are endless options and recipes, and this book will be a big help.

My Tips for Cooking with Duck

- Allowing time to rest the duck once you have cooked breasts or a whole bird is probably my best tip. This gives the meat time to relax and for any juices to be absorbed back into the duck, resulting in succulent, tender meat which carves easily. Some juices will be left on the plate, but you can use these to add extra flavour to your sauce or dressing. Resting times can vary but allow at least 10 minutes for duck breasts, 30 minutes for a whole duck and up to an hour with large birds like goose or turkey. I promise you will notice the difference.

- When cooking duck breast, I prefer a cold, unoiled pan placed on a low to medium heat so that the fat has longer to render (melt down) ensuring a golden brown crisp skin. Before cooking, dry the skin, lightly score with a sharp knife and season both sides with salt. I use table salt as it's easier to distribute evenly. Always start cooking duck breast skin side down in the pan.

- Saving the fat from roasting or rendering is also highly recommended, as it's great to use for making crispy, fluffy roast potatoes.

- Cooking duck or speciality poultry for guests can seem intimidating, so prepare as much as you can before they arrive. Many of our sauces can be prepared earlier in the day and then stored in the fridge. Warm them through in a pan on the hob when you are ready to serve your duck.

- Always remove meat from the fridge 30 to 60 minutes before cooking; this means the meat comes up to room temperature before you start cooking it, which reduces the amount of moisture that evaporates from the meat during the cooking process, resulting in a succulent roast.

- To help keep your oven clean, you can cover whole birds with foil while they roast and remove it around 30 minutes before the cooking time is up, so the skin has time to crisp up.

- Gressingham recommends that a whole duck serves two to four people (depending on the weight) and there are several ways to get as much use out of the bird as possible. Here are a few ideas:

- Save any uneaten meat and add it to a Thai curry, along with sweet potato to bulk it out if needed. You could also use it as a filling for crispy filo pastry parcels, Chinese pancakes or tortilla wraps. Serve with hoisin sauce for the perfect finish.

- Keep all the juices and fat from the roast. You can add the juices to your gravy or sauce and keep the fat for roast potatoes.

- Don't throw away the carcass! This can be frozen and then used to make soups, stock and gravy with real depth of flavour.

In short, cooking with duck is easier than you might think and will result in a memorable meal for you, your guests, family and friends. Enjoy trying out new flavours and discovering delicious dishes by following the hints and tips in this guide and, of course, our wonderful selection of recipes.

QUICK
AND

Duck Filo Rolls with Sweet Chilli and Lime Mayo

A great way to use up leftover duck from a Sunday roast.
Serve with a green salad for a dinner party starter or light lunch.

Makes: 9 | Preparation time: 30 minutes | Cooking time: 30 minutes

Ingredients

400g cooked shredded Gressingham duck

3 spring onions, thinly sliced

Small bunch of coriander, finely chopped

Thumb-sized piece of root ginger, peeled and grated

1 red chilli, finely diced (seeds optional)

2 tbsp mango chutney

2 tsp nigella seeds

Salt and pepper, to taste

1 packet of ready-made filo pastry (270g)

75g melted butter

200g good quality mayonnaise

3 tbsp sweet chilli sauce

½ a lime, zested and juiced

200ml vegetable oil

Method

Place the shredded duck into a bowl and combine it with the spring onions, coriander, ginger, chilli, mango chutney and nigella seeds. Season the mixture to taste.

Lay a sheet of filo pastry on a clean surface, brush with the melted butter, then lay another sheet on top. Cut the sheets into three evenly-sized rectangles. Repeat this process twice more to get nine double-layered rectangles of pastry.

Divide the duck mixture into nine portions. Spoon a portion onto one of the pastry rectangles, spreading it across one of the longest edges, leaving a gap at each end. Fold both the short sides inwards then roll up to form a cigar shape. Repeat with all the filling and pastry, then put the duck rolls into the fridge and chill for 1 hour before frying.

Meanwhile, combine the mayonnaise with the sweet chilli sauce and lime zest and juice, then transfer into a serving bowl and place in the fridge until needed.

When you're ready to cook the filo rolls, preheat the oven to 200°c or 180°c fan and put the vegetable oil into a non-stick frying pan on a medium heat. When the oil is hot, carefully place two or three rolls into the pan without crowding it. Using tongs, turn the rolls as they fry until golden on all sides. Repeat until all the rolls are done, then transfer them to a non-stick baking tray and finish cooking in the preheated oven for 8 to 10 minutes.

Serve the duck rolls with a green salad and the sweet chilli and lime mayonnaise for dipping.

Roast Duck Breast and Walnut Salad

This salad brings together a wonderful combination of textures and flavours,
from the crunchy bite of the walnuts to the juicy duck and crisp lettuce.
Enjoy with crusty bread and a glass of chilled rosé.

Serves: 4 as a starter, 2 as a main | Preparation time: 15 minutes | Cooking time: 30 minutes

Ingredients

8 new potatoes, unpeeled

2 Gressingham duck breasts

100g green beans, topped and tailed

1 bag of mixed salad leaves

2 little gem lettuces

50g walnuts, toasted

Small bunch of chives

For the French dressing

3 tbsp white wine vinegar

1 tbsp Dijon mustard

1 tbsp runny honey

6 tbsp olive oil

3 tbsp walnut oil

Method

First, make the dressing by whisking the vinegar, mustard, honey and a pinch of salt and pepper together. Whisk in the oils very slowly and then season to taste. Set aside.

Preheat your oven to 220°c or 200°c fan. Simmer the new potatoes in salted boiling water until tender. Dry the duck breasts with kitchen roll, then score the skin six to eight times with a sharp knife and season both sides. Place the duck breasts skin side down in a frying pan with no oil on a low to medium heat. Cook for 6 to 8 minutes or until the skin is golden and crisp. Carefully pour off any fat into a bowl as the duck cooks. Turn the breasts over and quickly seal the meat for 30 seconds. Transfer the duck to a roasting tray skin side down and place in the preheated oven. Cook for 6 to 8 minutes, or a few more if you prefer the duck well cooked.

Remove the duck from the oven and leave to rest for 5 to 10 minutes, skin side up, somewhere warm. Meanwhile, simmer the green beans in salted boiling water for 5 to 10 minutes until tender. Quickly whisk the dressing then dress the salad leaves, lettuce, beans and potatoes. Divide between two bowls. Carve the duck and arrange the slices on top. Sprinkle over the toasted walnuts and snip some chives over the top to finish.

Duck Steak
and Fries

Steak and chips done the Gressingham way. Best enjoyed with creamy homemade mayonnaise and dressed watercress.

Serves: 2 | Preparation time: 5 minutes | Cooking time: 20 minutes

Ingredients

2 Gressingham duck breasts

200g chips or fries

Method

Preheat the oven to 200°c or 180°c fan. Dry the duck breasts well with kitchen roll. Score the skin on each duck breast six to eight times and season well on both sides. Place the duck into a cold frying pan with no oil, skin side down on a low to medium heat.

Cook for about 6 to 8 minutes until the skin is golden and crisp, carefully pouring off any excess fat into a bowl as the duck cooks. Turn the breasts over and seal the meat for 30 seconds, then transfer them to a baking tray and place in the preheated oven for 6 to 8 minutes, or longer if you prefer duck well cooked.

When the duck is cooked to your liking, remove it from the oven and leave in a warm place to rest for 5 to 10 minutes. While the duck is resting, put your fries or chips on to cook, according to the instructions or your preferred method.

When you are ready to eat, carve the duck into thick slices and serve with the fries or chips.

Sticky Sweet Chilli Duck Legs

This sweet and lightly spicy sauce makes a perfect glaze.
Serve with a mango, cucumber and red onion salad.

Serves: 2 | Preparation time: 5 minutes | Cooking time: 1 hour 10 minutes

Ingredients

2 Gressingham duck legs

½ an orange

1 tsp salt

1 tsp caster sugar

½ tsp mild chilli powder

½ tsp Chinese five spice

½ tsp white pepper

3 tbsp sweet chilli sauce

Method

Preheat the oven to 180°c or 160°c fan. Dry the duck legs well with kitchen roll then lightly prick the skin with a cocktail stick. Squeeze the juice from the orange over them and rub in well. Combine the salt, sugar and spices then sprinkle the mixture over the duck legs and rub all over.

Place the duck in a deep baking tray and roast for 1 hour in the preheated oven. After this time, pour the chilli sauce over the legs and return to the oven for 10 minutes.

Remove the duck legs from the oven, baste well with the chilli sauce and juices, then serve on warm plates alongside steamed rice and vegetables of your choice.

By Abigail Buchanan

Crispy Duck Salad with Hoisin Dressing

This salad is simple to make and a great lunch dish or starter for dinner with friends. Feel free to swap out salad ingredients depending on what's in your fridge; for instance, this works equally well with other salad leaves or vegetables such as green beans and tenderstem broccoli.

Serves: 4 as a starter, 2 as a main | Preparation time: 15 minutes | Cooking time: 35-40 minutes

Ingredients

1 Gressingham aromatic half crispy duck

Salad leaves (rocket, baby spinach and finely shredded red or white cabbage work well)

2 medium carrots, grated

3 spring onions, finely chopped

½ cucumber, finely chopped

Pomegranate seeds, to serve (optional)

For the dressing

2 tbsp hoisin sauce

1 tbsp sesame oil

1-2 cloves of garlic, minced

1 lime, juiced

1 tsp freshly grated ginger

2 tsp soy sauce

1 red chilli, finely chopped

Salt and pepper, to taste

Method

Cook the duck according to the instructions on the packet. It will take between 35 and 40 minutes. While the duck is cooking, combine the ingredients for the dressing and mix well.

Combine the salad leaves, carrots, spring onions and cucumber in a large serving bowl. When the duck is cooked, leave it to stand for 10 minutes before shredding it.

Toss the shredded duck with the salad, drizzle over the dressing and serve scattered with pomegranate seeds.

Duck Scratchings

A tasty snack that is easy to prepare and also a great way of using up duck breast skin should it not be required for a recipe.

Serves: 2 | Preparation time: 10 minutes | Cooking time: 3 minutes

Ingredients

Skin of 2 Gressingham duck breast or legs

200ml duck fat or vegetable oil

Method

Using a sharp knife, halve the duck skins lengthways and widthways. Cut into 1cm slices then pat dry with kitchen paper.

Put the fat or oil in a small, deep pan on a medium heat and bring up to a temperature of 200°c (or test the temperature with a cube of bread; it should turn brown in 30 seconds when the oil is hot enough). Carefully lay the duck skin into the oil and fry until puffed up, golden and crispy.

Remove with a metal slotted spoon and place on clean kitchen paper. Immediately sprinkle over some salt, and for a little twist you could also sprinkle over some mild curry powder or Chinese five spice. Allow the duck scratchings to cool before eating.

Duck Breast with Balsamic Dressing and Cabbage

Our famous one pan duck dish, with a beautiful balance of sweet, sour and salty flavour.
A delicious recipe, and it saves on the washing up!

Serves: 2 | Preparation time: 10 minutes | Cooking time: 30 minutes

Ingredients

200g new potatoes

2 Gressingham duck breasts

Sea salt

1 tsp black peppercorns, crushed

1 small bunch of flat-leaf parsley, roughly chopped

1 clove of garlic, finely chopped

3 rashers of smoked streaky bacon, thickly sliced

½ a small savoy cabbage, trimmed, quartered, cored and finely sliced

1 tbsp apple balsamic vinegar

2 tbsp olive oil

Method

Preheat your oven to 220°c or 200°c fan. Simmer the potatoes in boiling salted water for 10 minutes until tender. Drain, cool and thickly slice.

Dry the duck breasts well with kitchen roll. Score the skin of the duck six to eight times with a sharp knife. Season well with salt and pepper. Place the duck skin side down in a cold non-stick frying pan with no oil over a low to medium heat. Cook for 6 to 8 minutes until the skin is golden and crispy. Carefully pour off any excess fat into a bowl as the duck cooks. Turn over and seal the meat for 30 seconds. Transfer the duck breasts onto a baking tray, skin side down, and place in the preheated oven to roast for 6 to 8 minutes.

Remove the duck from the oven and allow it to rest for 5 to 10 minutes somewhere warm. While the duck is resting, place the frying pan over a high heat and add the sliced potato. Fry until brown and crisp. Scatter over the parsley and garlic. Transfer the potatoes to a warm plate and season with sea salt.

Keep the pan on the heat and fry the bacon until crisp before adding the cabbage. Stir fry for 1 minute, then add a splash of water and cook for 5 minutes until the cabbage has wilted.

Whisk any juices from the rested duck with the balsamic vinegar and olive oil for the dressing. Carve the duck breast into thick slices. Divide the cabbage, bacon and potatoes between two warm plates, place the duck slices on top and drizzle over the dressing.

Duck à l'orange

Our modern twist on an old favourite, a classic of the 1960s. Chicory has a slight bitterness that goes very well with the sweet orange sauce.

Serves: 2 | Preparation time: 20 minutes | Cooking time: 20 minutes

Ingredients

2 Gressingham duck breasts

2 large oranges

Salt and black pepper

200g new potatoes

1 spring onion

1 tbsp butter

2 heads of chicory

1 tsp caster sugar

250ml hot chicken stock (homemade or from bouillon)

1 star anise

1 tsp cornflour

Method

Dry the duck breasts well with kitchen roll. Lightly score the skin six to eight times with a sharp knife. Zest one of the oranges and rub half of the zest into the duck breasts along with a good pinch of salt.

Cut the potatoes into quarters and simmer them in boiling salted water for 10 minutes or until tender. Drain and keep warm in the pan by covering them with a lid.

Meanwhile, peel one of the oranges and put the segments in a bowl, then squeeze the juice from the other orange into the same bowl. Preheat your oven to 200°c or 180°c fan.

Top and tail the spring onion and chop into slim slices. Crush the cooked potatoes lightly with a fork, add the spring onion along with a quarter of a teaspoon of salt, a grind of pepper and the tablespoon of butter. Cover and keep warm. Halve both the heads of chicory lengthways.

Put the duck breasts skin side down in a cold frying pan without oil on a low to medium heat. Cook for 6 to 8 minutes or until the skin is crisp and golden. Carefully pour off any excess fat into a bowl as you cook. Transfer the duck breasts to a baking tray, skin side up, place into the preheated oven and cook for 6 minutes, or longer if you prefer your duck well cooked.

Using the same frying pan, warm one tablespoon of the reserved duck fat over a high heat, then cook the chicory cut side down for 5 minutes until golden. Sprinkle in the sugar, turn the chicory over a couple of times, then add the hot stock. Bring to a boil, cover, turn the heat down and simmer for 5 to 8 minutes until the chicory has softened. Transfer the chicory to a warm dish.

Pour the orange juice into the pan, add the star anise and keep it bubbling over a medium heat for a couple of minutes. Mix the cornflour with one teaspoon of water to make a slurry, then whisk it into the juice. Add the orange segments and simmer for a further minute.

Carve the duck into six to eight slices on an angle, then serve with the chicory, orange sauce and crushed new potatoes.

Duck Breast with Sweet Potato Mash

This quick and easy supper dish is perfect as an end of the week treat and proves that cooking with duck is not as difficult as you may think. This eats well with buttered greens.

Serves: 2 | Preparation time: 10 minutes | Cooking time: 30 minutes

Ingredients

200g sweet potatoes, peeled and cut into chunks

2 Gressingham duck breasts

Knob of butter

½ tsp ground nutmeg

Salt and black pepper

Handful of fresh coriander leaves, roughly chopped

Method

Preheat the oven to 220°c or 200°c fan. Simmer the sweet potatoes in salted water until tender, which should take about 10 to 15 minutes.

Meanwhile, prepare the duck. Dry the duck breasts well with kitchen roll. Score the skin six to eight times with a sharp knife and season on both sides.

Place the duck breasts skin side down in a non-stick pan without oil on a low to medium heat. Cook for 6 to 8 minutes until the skin is golden and crisp, pouring off any excess fat into a bowl as the duck cooks. Turn the breasts over and quickly seal the meat for 30 seconds.

Transfer the duck to a deep roasting tray, skin side down, and place in the preheated oven for 6 to 8 minutes, or longer if you prefer your duck well cooked. When done to your liking, remove the duck from the oven and leave it to rest somewhere warm for 5 to 10 minutes.

Drain the boiled sweet potato well, return it to the pan and then mash with the butter and nutmeg along with salt and pepper to taste. Garnish with fresh coriander.

Duck Noodle Soup

Try this delicious noodle soup full of our favourite Eastern flavours and textures. We use the half aromatic duck for this but you can use any leftover roast duck, or it also works well with chicken.

Serves: 2 | Preparation time: 30 minutes | Cooking time: 30 minutes

Ingredients

1 Gressingham half aromatic duck

150g rice vermicelli noodles

1 tbsp vegetable oil

1 thumb-sized piece of ginger, peeled and finely sliced

1 clove of garlic, peeled and finely chopped

2 spring onions, finely sliced

1 litre chicken stock (homemade or from bouillon)

1½ tbsp oyster sauce

1 tbsp light soy sauce

2 pak choi, quartered lengthways

1 red chilli, finely sliced

1 spring onion, finely sliced

Method

Preheat the oven to 200°c or 180°c fan. Remove any packaging from the aromatic duck, place it on a baking tray and cook in the preheated oven for 30 minutes.

While the duck is cooking, prepare the soup. First, cook the noodles as per the packet instructions, refresh them in cold water then drain and set aside.

Heat the oil in a deep pan then gently fry the ginger, garlic and spring onions until softened. Pour in the hot chicken stock, oyster sauce and soy sauce, then simmer on a low heat until the duck is ready. Season to taste.

When the duck has roasted, remove it from the oven and shred the meat from the bones with two forks. Bring the soup up to boil and blanch the pak choi for 2 minutes, then remove carefully with tongs. Do the same with the noodles.

Now divide the noodles and pak choi between two warm bowls and top with the shredded duck.

Ladle over the hot soup then garnish with the chilli and spring onions.

Duck Stir Fry with Oyster Sauce

Stir fries are a tasty midweek meal, and the rich flavour of the duck
works perfectly with these zingy oriental flavours.

Serves: 2 | Preparation time: 15 minutes | Cooking time: 15 minutes

Ingredients

300g medium egg noodles

1 pack of Gressingham stir fry strips

1 tsp sesame oil

1 tsp light soy sauce

1 red onion, sliced

½ red pepper, sliced

2cm ginger, peeled and finely chopped

1 clove of garlic, finely chopped

1 tbsp oyster sauce

120ml chicken stock or water

1 spring onion, finely sliced

Handful of coriander leaves, roughly chopped

Method

Cook the noodles according to the packet instructions then refresh them
in cold water. Strain in a colander, lightly toss in a little sesame oil then
set aside.

Mix the duck stir fry strips with the sesame oil and soy sauce. Heat a wok
or frying pan with a little vegetable oil. When the wok or pan begins to
smoke, carefully add the duck and stir fry for 2 to 3 minutes until nearly
cooked through and browned off. Remove from the wok and set aside.

Add a little more oil to the wok and stir fry the onion and pepper for 1
minute before adding the ginger and garlic. Stir fry for another minute, then
add the oyster sauce and 30ml of the stock or water. Cook for 2 more
minutes, adding more stock or water when the sauce becomes sticky.

Return the duck to the wok along with the noodles and spring onions.
Lightly season the stir fry and cook for a further 2 minutes, ensuring
the ingredients are well mixed and adding stock as necessary. Serve
immediately and garnish with the fresh coriander.

Tamarind and Ginger Duck Breast

Try this spicy, rich sauce to give your duck a sweet and sour flavour.
Serve with noodles or steamed rice and pak choi.

Serves: 2 | Preparation time: 5 minutes | Cooking time: 20 minutes

Ingredients

2 Gressingham duck breasts

Salt and ground black pepper

1 tbsp Chinese five spice

1 tbsp dried thyme

1 tbsp vegetable oil

2 tbsp finely chopped garlic

4 tbsp finely diced ginger

6 tbsp tamarind purée

2 tbsp oyster sauce

2 tbsp fish sauce

4 tbsp caster sugar

100ml duck or chicken stock or water

Method

Preheat the oven to 180°c or 160°c fan. Dry the duck breasts with kitchen paper and score the fat six to eight times on each one. Season well with the salt, pepper, Chinese five spice and thyme.

Place the duck breasts skin side down in a large frying pan on a medium heat without any oil. Cook for approximately 8 minutes until the fat has rendered out and the skin has turned golden brown and crisp. While cooking, pour off the excess rendered fat to help this happen. Turn the duck breasts over to briefly seal the other side, then transfer them to a roasting tin and place in the preheated oven for 8 minutes.

While the duck is roasting, pour off most of any remaining fat from the frying pan and add the vegetable oil, garlic and ginger. Cook on a medium heat, stirring constantly without colouring. Add the tamarind, oyster sauce, fish sauce, and sugar then cook until dissolved. Stir in the stock and bring to a simmer. Once your sauce is the consistency of a thick glaze, season to taste with salt and pepper.

Remove the duck breasts from the oven and rest on a warm plate for 7 to 10 minutes. Carve, then arrange on a hot plate and drizzle with the tamarind and ginger sauce.

Crispy Aromatic Duck Pancakes

Make your own version of this Chinese classic with marinated and slow cooked
duck legs garnished with spring onions, cucumber and, of course, hoisin sauce.

Serves: 4-6 | Preparation time: 10 minutes, plus overnight marinating | Cooking time: 1 hour 35 minutes

Ingredients

4 Gressingham duck legs

2 star anise

2 sticks of cinnamon

1 tsp szechuan peppercorns (or black peppercorns if unavailable)

1 tsp cloves

6 tbsp Chinese rice wine (or dry sherry)

8 tbsp light soy sauce

8 tbsp soft brown sugar

3 tsp salt

3cm fresh ginger, sliced

4 spring onions

1.2 litres chicken stock or water

To serve

Chinese pancakes

Spring onions, sliced into matchsticks

Cucumber, sliced into matchsticks

Hoisin or plum sauce

Method

Stir all the ingredients except the duck legs together in a large saucepan.
Add the duck legs to the pan so they are submerged, cover and refrigerate
overnight.

When you are ready to cook, place the pan containing the marinated duck
over a high heat and bring to the boil. Turn down the heat to a gentle
simmer and cook for 1 hour 15 minutes or until the meat easily comes
away from the bone.

Remove the duck legs from the liquor to drain, then place the legs under a
hot grill until the skin goes crispy. You can also do this in a very hot (220°c)
oven for 10 minutes.

Carefully place the duck legs on a hot dish. Using two forks, take off the
crispy skin and shred the meat from the bones. Serve with warm Chinese
pancakes, spring onions, cucumber and hoisin or plum sauce.

Five Spice Duck Leg and Asian Slaw

A perfect summer recipe for enjoying outdoors in the sunshine.
The Asian slaw has a punchy dressing that livens up the vegetables.

Serves: 2 | Preparation time: 10 minutes | Cooking time: 1 hour 15 minutes

Ingredients

2 Gressingham duck legs

1 tsp Chinese five spice

Salt and black pepper

For the Asian slaw

1 carrot, grated

½ small red cabbage, grated

1 large red or yellow pepper, finely sliced

½ onion, finely sliced

1 clove of garlic, finely chopped

Thumb-sized piece of root ginger, peeled and finely chopped

1 tsp sesame oil

1 tbsp fish sauce

1 lime, zested and juiced

Large handful of mixed salad leaves

Method

Preheat the oven to 180°c or 180°c fan. Prick the skin of the duck legs all over, then season well with the Chinese five spice plus salt and pepper.

Place the prepared duck legs on a baking tray, skin side up, and roast in the preheated oven for about 1 hour 15 minutes, checking after 1 hour, until tender and caramelised.

For the Asian slaw

While the duck is cooking, prepare the slaw by combining the carrot, red cabbage, pepper, onion and garlic in a large mixing bowl. Add the ginger, sesame oil, fish sauce, lime zest and juice, and the salad leaves to the bowl with the vegetables. Season to taste and then toss everything together.

To serve, divide the Asian slaw between two plates and place the duck legs on top.

Duck and Pak Choi Noodles

A delicious midweek treat, ready in just twenty minutes! This fresh and colourful dish
is full of healthy vegetables and contrasting textures.

Serves: 2 | Preparation time: 10 minutes | Cooking time: 10 minutes

Ingredients

1 Gressingham duck breast

300g medium egg noodles

1 tbsp vegetable oil

1 red onion, finely sliced

2 cloves of garlic, peeled and finely chopped

2cm fresh ginger, peeled and grated

1 red chilli, finely sliced

1 red pepper, finely sliced

1 courgette, halved lengthways and sliced at
an angle

2 pak choi, leaves separated

1 tbsp honey

100ml chicken stock or water

1 tbsp light soy sauce

1 tsp sesame oil

Method

Take the skin off the duck breast and slice the meat into strips. Cook
the noodles according to the instructions on the packet. Strain through a
colander and lightly toss in a little oil.

Heat the wok over a medium heat and add the vegetable oil. Once
smoking, add the duck and stir fry for 2 to 3 minutes until cooked through
and browned off. Lightly season the meat, remove it from the wok and
set aside.

Add a little more oil to the wok and stir fry the onion, garlic, ginger and
chilli for 1 minute. Add the pepper and courgette then stir fry for another
minute.

Then add the cooked noodles, pak choi, honey and stock or water to the
wok. Toss everything together using tongs until the pak choi wilts and the
noodles are steaming hot. Return the cooked duck to the wok, mix it in
and finish with the soy sauce and sesame oil.

Stir well and serve in warm bowls.

Hoisin and Soy Roasted Duck Platter

This goes well with Chinese pancakes, similar to Peking duck. It also can be made for two to three people with two duck legs and half of the other ingredients. A great sharing meal.

Serves: 4-5 | Preparation time: 15 minutes | Cooking time: 2 hours

Ingredients

For the duck stock

1 whole Gressingham duck

140ml Chinese rice wine or dry sherry

5 tbsp light soy sauce

5 tbsp hoisin sauce

3 cloves of garlic, crushed

2 thumb-sized pieces of root ginger, sliced

2 tsp Chinese five spice

2 tbsp sugar

For the noodles

250g egg noodles

1 tbsp sesame oil

1 small red pepper, finely chopped

1 clove of garlic, finely chopped

2 spring onions, finely sliced

1 tbsp light soy sauce

For the garnish

1 cucumber, peeled and cut into ribbons

2 spring onions, finely sliced

Method

Preheat your oven to 180°c or 160°c fan. Remove the duck from its packaging, pat dry and if there are giblets in the cavity, remove them. Place the duck into a large saucepan and cover with cold water. Bring to the boil and simmer for about 20 minutes.

Carefully transfer the duck into a large deep sided roasting tray. Measure out 600ml of the poaching water in a large jug, then stir in all the duck stock ingredients. Ladle this stock over the duck in the roasting tin. Loosely cover with foil and place in the preheated oven.

Cook for 1 hour 30 minutes, turning and basting the duck every 30 minutes. If the duck is not tender after this time, keep roasting but check every 15 minutes until the leg bones pull away easily. Remove the duck from the oven and leave it to rest while you prepare the noodles.

Cook the noodles according to the instructions on the packet. Drain and set aside. Place a wok or non-stick frying pan on a medium to high heat and add the sesame oil, followed by the red pepper, garlic and spring onion. Stir fry for 30 seconds then add the cooked noodles. Stir fry for another 30 seconds then add the soy sauce. Fry for a final 2 minutes, then it's ready to serve.

Place the roasted duck onto a platter, surround it with the noodles and then garnish with the remaining spring onion and the cucumber ribbons. Shred the duck meat off the bones with two forks and help yourselves to this delicious Chinese classic.

Twice Cooked Duck Stir Fry with Black Bean Sauce

Reproduce a Cantonese classic at home with this easy-to-follow recipe. In this version we pan fry the duck breast first before starting our stir fry. Serve with steamed rice.

Serves: 2 | Preparation time: 20 minutes | Cooking time: 30 minutes

Ingredients

2 Gressingham duck breasts

2 tbsp vegetable oil

I onion, peeled and finely sliced

I large red or yellow pepper, cored, halved and sliced

2 cloves of garlic, peeled and finely chopped

Thumb-sized piece of root ginger, peeled and finely sliced

2 tsp fermented black beans (or 250ml shop-bought black bean sauce)

I tbsp light soy

Handful of baby spinach

I chilli, finely sliced (optional)

I tsp blended sesame oil

2 spring onions, finely sliced

Method

Dry the duck breasts well with kitchen paper. Lightly score the skin with a sharp knife six to eight times. Lightly season both sides.

Lay the duck breasts skin side down in a cold frying pan with no oil on a low to medium heat. Cook for 8 to 10 minutes until the skin is crisp and golden. Carefully pour off any excess fat into a bowl, then turn the duck breasts over to seal the meat and cook for a further 2 minutes. Take the pan off the heat and leave the duck to rest.

Heat the oil in a wok or large frying pan until hot. Put the onion and pepper into the wok and stir fry for 2 minutes. Add the garlic and ginger then cook for a further I minute, adding a touch of water if anything is sticking.

Add the black beans (or ready-made sauce if using) and soy sauce, stir fry for 2 minutes, then turn the heat down low.

Carve the rested duck into thin slices, pour any juices into the wok, turn the heat back up and add the duck, spinach, chilli (if using) and sesame oil to the wok. Stir fry for 2 minutes, again adding a little water if required. Taste to check the seasoning, divide the stir fry between two plates and garnish with the spring onions to serve.

Thai Duck Salad with Lime, Chilli and Garlic Dressing

Thai beef salad is a classic and rightly so. Using duck instead is just as tasty.
If you'd like a milder dressing, remove the seeds from the chilli.

Serves: 2 | Preparation time: 20 minutes | Cooking time: 30 minutes

Ingredients

1 large or 2 small Gressingham duck breasts

Handful of salad leaves, washed

Few mint leaves, roughly torn

1 tomato, cut into wedges

1 lime, cut into wedges

½ tsp sesame seeds

For the dressing

1 clove of garlic, peeled and finely chopped

1 small chilli, finely chopped

½ a lime, juiced

1 tbsp fish sauce

2 tsp water

2 tsp sugar

Dash of blended sesame oil

Method

Preheat the oven to 200°c or 180°c fan. Dry the duck breasts well with kitchen paper. Lightly score the skin with a sharp knife six to eight times. Season both sides with salt and pepper.

Lay the duck breasts skin side down into a cold frying pan without oil, then cook over a low to medium heat for about 6 to 8 minutes until the skin is golden and crispy. Carefully drain off any fat into a bowl as you go.

Turn the duck breasts over to seal the meat for 30 seconds and then transfer to a baking tray skin side up and place in the preheated oven for 8 minutes, or longer if you prefer your duck more well done. Meanwhile, put all the dressing ingredients in a bowl and stir well to combine everything. Arrange the salad leaves, mint, wedges of tomato and lime on two serving plates.

Remove the duck from the oven when cooked to your liking, then leave it to rest for at least 10 minutes on a warm plate. After resting, slice the duck and place it neatly on top of the salad. Stir any juices from the duck into the dressing, then spoon the dressing over the duck and sprinkle over the sesame seeds to finish.

DATE
NIGHT

By Uğur Vata, chef patron of The Galley, Woodbridge

Sautéed Duck with Figs and Pomegranate

Rich duck legs with new season Turkish black figs and pomegranate is a wonderful combination. Serve with mashed potato and your favourite seasonal vegetables.

Serves: 2 | Preparation time: 5 minutes | Cooking time: 70 minutes

Ingredients

50g unsalted butter

2 Gressingham duck legs

Sea salt and freshly ground black pepper

100ml chicken stock

75ml pomegranate molasses

4 fresh black figs, quartered

1 pomegranate

Method

Preheat the oven to 180°c or 160°c fan.

Put the butter in a frying pan over a high heat. When the butter foam subsides, lay the duck legs skin side down in the pan. Cook them briefly on both sides, less than 10 minutes in total, season, then transfer the duck legs to an oven proof dish and into the preheated oven for 1 hour.

While the duck legs are cooking put the chicken stock and pomegranate molasses in the frying pan and let them simmer briskly over a medium heat for about 2 to 3 minutes, scraping loose any residue from cooking the duck on the bottom and sides of the pan.

When the duck legs are cooked place the quartered figs in the sauce with the legs. Turn them two or three times to cover in sauce, then remove the duck. Serve on warm plates scattered with pomegranate seeds (remove these by halving the pomegranate, holding it over a bowl and rapping the skin with a spoon) and surrounded by the figs and pomegranate sauce.

Honey and Orange Glazed Duck Breast

A deliciously sweet and fruity recipe that's quick and simple to prepare. The flavourful duck and potatoes just need a few mixed leaves or some buttered spinach to accompany them.

Serves: 2 | Preparation time: 10 minutes | Cooking time: 25 minutes

Ingredients

- 2 Gressingham duck breasts
- 2 large oranges
- 6-8 large new potatoes, halved
- 120g runny honey
- 2 cloves of garlic, thinly sliced
- 3 large sprigs of thyme

Method

Preheat the oven to 180°c or 160°c fan. Dry the duck well with kitchen roll and score the skin six to eight times with a sharp knife. Peel and segment one of the oranges. Zest the other orange and squeeze the juice out into a bowl.

Season the duck with salt and place into a cold pan skin side down with no oil over a low to medium heat. Cook for 6 to 8 minutes until the skin is crispy and golden. Carefully pour any excess fat into a bowl as it renders down. Turn the duck over and seal the meat for 30 seconds, then transfer the duck breasts to a baking tray skin side up. Place them in the preheated oven for 5 minutes.

Simmer the potatoes in boiling salted water for 5 to 10 minutes until just softened. Meanwhile, place the pan used for the duck back on the heat and add the honey, orange juice and zest, all the garlic and half the thyme. Stir everything together and boil to reduce the sauce by half. Add the potatoes and orange segments to the pan, then simmer until the sauce has a sticky glaze consistency. Keep warm while you finish the duck.

Remove the duck from the oven and glaze the skin generously with some of the sauce. Return it to the oven for 2 to 3 minutes if you like it rare, or cook for a few minutes longer if you prefer it well cooked. Remove and allow to rest for 5 to 10 minutes somewhere warm.

When you are ready to eat, bring the pan of sauce and potatoes back to a simmer on a medium heat. Divide the sauce and potatoes between two warm plates. Carve the duck breasts into five or six pieces and place on top. Garnish with the remaining thyme.

Pulled Duck and Sweet Chilli

If you like classic Tex-Mex pulled pork, then you will love this spicy, rich duck version.
Best served with lots of crusty bread and creamy homemade slaw.

Serves: 2 | Preparation time: 5 minutes | Cooking time: 1 hour 25 minutes

Ingredients

2 Gressingham duck legs

½ tsp ground cumin

½ tsp paprika

200g sweet chilli sauce

2 large handfuls of salad leaves

2 spring onions, finely chopped

Method

Preheat the oven to 180°c or 160°c fan. Season the duck legs with salt and pepper on both sides. Mix the cumin and paprika together in a bowl and rub into the legs.

Place the duck legs on a wire rack in a baking tray and put in them in the preheated oven. Cook for about 1 hour 10 minutes, then remove them from the oven and lower the temperature to 150°c or 130°c fan. Transfer the duck legs to a clean roasting tray and baste them with the chilli sauce. Return to the oven for another 15 minutes.

Take the duck legs out of the oven and allow them to cool until you can handle them. Shred the duck meat and skin from the bones with two forks.

Divide the salad leaves between two plates and top with the shredded sweet chilli duck. Garnish with the sliced spring onions and more sweet chilli sauce.

Duck Legs
with Plum Sauce

A traditional duck recipe that is truly delicious. It goes well with roasted butternut squash and buttered greens, but you could serve it with mashed potato.

Serves: 2 | Preparation time: 10 minutes | Cooking time: 1 hour

Ingredients

2 Gressingham duck legs

Vegetable oil

2 or 3 plums, stoned and roughly chopped

100ml red wine

½ star anise (optional)

300ml beef stock

2 or 3 dessert spoons of plum jam

Method

Preheat your oven to 190°c or 170°c fan. Pat the duck legs dry with absorbent paper and season both sides with salt. Place them on a wire rack over a roasting tin (a grill pan would work) and pour half a glass of water into the tin. Place in the preheated oven for 1 hour 10 minutes. Check the meat for tenderness and return to the oven for a further 10 minutes if necessary. While the duck is cooking, prepare the sauce and your choice of vegetables.

Place a saucepan on a high heat with a dessert spoon of vegetable oil. When it's hot, add the plums and cook until coloured and slightly softened (about 2 minutes). Pour in the wine and star anise (if using) then reduce the liquid by a third. Add the stock and jam, stir in and simmer for 10 minutes, then set the sauce aside in a warm place. If the sauce is too thin, mix a teaspoon of cornflour with a little cold water and stir the paste thoroughly into the sauce.

Serve the roasted duck legs on warm plates glazed with the hot plum sauce, alongside your chosen vegetables. My favorite way to serve this dish is with roasted butternut squash and simple greens.

Moroccan Duck Salad

This wonderful salad benefits from the sweet smoky flavours of the rose harissa. It is still delicious without, if spice is not your preference.

Serves: 2 | Preparation time: 15 minutes, plus 1 hour marinating | Cooking time: 30 minutes

Ingredients

2 Gressingham duck breasts, skin removed

2 tbsp rose harissa paste (optional)

6 tbsp good olive oil

2 aubergines, sliced into 1cm thick rounds

50g pine nuts

2 gem lettuce, separated into leaves and washed

100g feta cheese, crumbled

1 bunch of flat leaf parsley, roughly chopped

½ a lemon, juiced

1 tsp honey

Method

Coat the duck breasts in the rose harissa paste and two tablespoons of the olive oil. Leave the duck to marinate for 1 hour.

Preheat the oven to 200°c or 180°c fan, and put a griddle on a high heat. Sear your marinated duck for 2 minutes on each side, then transfer it to a baking tray and place in the preheated oven to finish cooking for 8 minutes.

Brush the aubergine slices with a little olive oil and season. Using the same pan you used to sear the duck, griddle the aubergine in small batches, turning once when they are charred. Transfer to a warm plate lined with kitchen towel to absorb excess oil.

Remove the duck from the oven and leave it to rest for 10 minutes before carving into thick slices. Meanwhile, toast the pine nuts either in the warm oven or a clean dry pan on the hob.

To serve

Cover a large plate with the gem lettuce leaves, arrange the warm aubergine on top then sprinkle over the feta cheese and chopped parsley. Make a quick dressing with the lemon juice, honey, remaining olive oil and seasoning. Drizzle this over the salad then top with the sliced duck breast and toasted pine nuts.

Whole Roast Guinea Fowl with Roasted Root Vegetables

A simple but tasty supper for a cosy night in.
Great served with sourdough for mopping up the pan juices.

Serves: 2 | Preparation time: 15 minutes | Cooking time: 1 hour 20 minutes

Ingredients

200g new potatoes, cleaned and halved

1 red onion, peeled and cut into wedges

1 large carrot, peeled, quartered and cut into 5cm lengths

1 medium parsnip, peeled and quartered

1 bulb of garlic, cut in half horizontally

Salt and black pepper

4 tbsp olive oil

1 Gressingham guinea fowl

A few sprigs of thyme

200ml boiling water

250g green beans, topped and tailed

Method

Preheat the oven to 180°c or 160°c fan.

Place all the prepared vegetables (except the green beans) and the garlic in a deep sided roasting dish. Season well, pour over the olive oil and mix everything together.

Season the guinea fowl and place it on top of the vegetables. Scatter the thyme over the top and pour the water into the dish. Cover with foil and place in the preheated oven to roast.

After 1 hour, remove the foil, adjust the oven temperature to 200°c and cook for a further 15 minutes.

Use the remaining time to cook the beans. Simmer the green beans in salted boiling water for 4 minutes, then drain.

Take the roasting dish out of the oven and remove the foil. Transfer the guinea fowl to a plate for carving, then stir the beans into the other vegetables and pile them into a dish. Your meal is now ready to serve. Place everything in the middle of the table for your guests to share.

By Maurice and Miriam Buchanan, Gressingham's founders

Duck Breast with Cherries

An elegant yet simple main course for a romantic supper, or double it up to cook for friends.
Perfect with roasted vegetables. Defrosted cherries are fine but require less cooking so add
them near the end.

Serves: 2 | Preparation time: 15 minutes | Cooking time: 20-30 minutes

Ingredients

2 Gressingham duck breasts

1 long shallot, peeled and finely sliced

Handful of fresh cherries, pitted

50ml good Port

100ml rich chicken stock

1 tbsp runny honey

1 sprig of fresh thyme

Method

Preheat your oven to 200°c or 180°c fan. Dry the duck breasts well on kitchen paper. Lightly score the skin with a sharp knife six to eight times along the duck breast (to help the fat render out and flavour the meat). Season well with salt and pepper.

Lay the duck breasts skin side down into a cold, unoiled frying pan. Cook over a low-medium heat for about 6 to 8 minutes until the skin is golden and crispy (while regularly draining off any fat carefully into a bowl). Turn the duck breasts over to seal the meat side for 30 seconds and then transfer them to a roasting tray (keep the frying pan for later).

Cook the duck in the oven for 10 to 20 minutes (depending on how well done you like it). Transfer the duck to a hot plate and rest somewhere warm for 10 minutes while you prepare the sauce.

Heat up the frying pan with a little of the duck fat over a medium heat. Add the shallot and cherries, stir frying them until softened. Add the remaining ingredients and turn up the heat to full, boiling the pan's contents until the liquid becomes thickened and syrupy, stirring occasionally to make sure nothing sticks to the pan.

Carve the duck thickly and serve glazed with the cherries and the sauce.

By Amie Elizabeth White, Gressingham customer

Roasted Duck Legs with Figs and Choucroute

This interesting dish is best enjoyed in the peak season for figs, so in the UK that means late summer or early autumn. We enjoy it with a dressed rocket leaf salad alongside the choucroute.

Serves: 2 | Preparation time: 10 minutes | Cooking time: 1 hour 15 minutes

Ingredients

2 Gressingham duck legs

For the choucroute

Good knob of butter

250g sauerkraut, drained

2 bay leaves

1 tsp dried thyme

1 tsp black pepper

200ml white wine

100ml stock

For the figs and shallots

Olive oil

2 medium shallots, peeled and thinly sliced

4 fresh figs, stalk removed and quartered

100ml good stock (preferably veal)

Hazelnut oil

Hazelnuts, for garnish

Method

Preheat your oven to 180°c or 160°c fan. Dry the duck legs with paper towels before pricking the skin all over with a fork and seasoning with salt and pepper. Place them in a shallow roasting tin on the middle shelf of the preheated oven. Set a timer for 1 hour 30 minutes and baste the legs regularly while they roast.

For the choucroute

Add a good knob of butter to a large saucepan and place on a high heat. Once melted and bubbling, add the drained sauerkraut, bay leaves, thyme, black pepper and white wine. Stir fry for a few minutes before adding the stock. Bring back to a simmer and then cover with a lid. Leave on a very low heat, stirring occasionally.

For the figs and shallots

Sauté the shallots in a hot frying pan with a little oil over a medium to high heat. As they start to caramelise, fold in the figs then remove the pan from the heat.

Around 20 minutes before the duck roasting time is up, bring the stock to a simmer in a saucepan. Next, drain off most of the fat from the roasting tin and pour in the hot stock along with the shallots and figs around the duck legs. Stir everything together gently. Return the tin to the oven and continue roasting with the heat increased to 200°c or 180°c fan for another 15 minutes.

Serve the duck legs on a bed of choucroute with the figs and shallots scattered around along with a spoonful or two of the pan juices. To finish, drizzle with a little hazelnut oil.

Duck Panang Curry

Get creative with those leftovers from your Sunday roast with this aromatic red Thai curry. It's traditionally made with pork but this recipe uses delicious duck. You can also use leftover roast potatoes, added at the same time as the duck (instead of raw potatoes as below).

Serves: 4 | Preparation time: 10 minutes | Cooking time: 30 minutes

Ingredients

1 medium onion, peeled and sliced

2 large potatoes, peeled and cut into chunks

Vegetable oil

1 tbsp red Thai curry paste

1 tin of coconut milk

4 lime leaves

1 tbsp palm or brown sugar

1 tbsp fish sauce

1 head of pak choi, leaves separated and cleaned

500g cooked shredded Gressingham duck

2 tbsp roasted peanuts

1 lime, halved

Fresh coriander

Thai basil

Method

Soften the onion and potato in a deep pan over a medium heat with a little oil for 5 minutes. Add the curry paste and coconut milk then bring to the boil.

Stir in the lime leaves, sugar and fish sauce then simmer until the potato is almost cooked. Roughly chop the pak choi and add it to the pan along with the duck and the peanuts. Heat through until steaming.

Squeeze over the juice of half the lime, stir and then adjust the seasoning to taste. Garnish with fresh coriander and Thai basil then serve with basmati rice and the remaining lime.

Duck Breast with Tomato and Basil Pasta

This sweet, piquant dish never fails to impress and is a favourite way of preparing Gressingham duck.

Serves: 2 | Preparation time: 5 minutes | Cooking time: 30 minutes

Ingredients

2 Gressingham duck breasts

½ a lemon, zested

1 tbsp rapeseed oil

150g spaghetti

2 tbsp olive oil

1 clove of garlic, peeled and finely chopped

150g baby plum tomatoes, halved

Handful of fresh basil

50g parmesan, finely grated

Method

Preheat your oven to 200°c or 180°c fan. Lightly score the skin of the duck breasts six to eight times without cutting the meat underneath.

Place the duck breasts skin side down into a non-stick pan on a medium heat. Cook until the skin is golden, which should take about 3 minutes, before turning over to seal the meat on the other side.

Transfer the duck breasts skin side down to a baking tray and roast them in the preheated oven for 10 to 12 minutes, longer if you like your duck well done. Leave to rest for 10 minutes somewhere warm.

Cook the spaghetti as per the packet instructions. Drain well and reserve a little pasta water. Heat the olive oil in a non-stick frying pan on a low to medium heat and add the finely chopped garlic. Cook for 1 minute, then add the tomatoes with two tablespoons of the reserved pasta water. Cook for 3 minutes, then add the cooked spaghetti to the pan with another tablespoon of pasta water, a squeeze of lemon juice and most of the basil. Lightly season.

Toss the pasta so everything is combined, then divide between two warm plates or bowls. Carve each duck breast into six slices and place them on top of the spaghetti. Finish with the grated parmesan and remaining basil then serve immediately.

Roast Duck Legs with Blackberry and Port Sauce

Served with sautéed potatoes, curly kale, and sticky shallots. A delicious duck recipe
for a date night dinner or Valentine's Day.

Serves: 2 | Preparation time: 20 minutes | Cooking time: 1 hour 15 minutes

Ingredients

2 Gressingham duck legs

8 new potatoes, unpeeled

1 large bunch of curly kale, roughly chopped
and stalks removed

4 shallots

1 tbsp soft brown sugar

1 tbsp balsamic vinegar

5-6 tbsp rapeseed oil

For the sauce

350ml Port

400ml chicken stock or water

1 punnet of blackberries

1 tbsp balsamic vinegar

1 star anise

2 tsp white sugar

1 tsp cornflour, mixed with a little water to
form a paste

50g butter

Method

Preheat your oven to 180°c or 160°c fan. Pat the duck legs with kitchen
roll or a clean tea towel to remove excess moisture, then prick the skin
all over. Season with salt and pepper, then place the duck legs on a wire
rack in a roasting tray and cook in the middle of the preheated oven for 1
hour 15 minutes.

While the duck is cooking, boil the potatoes in a pan of water for
10 minutes, then scoop them out and leave to cool on a paper lined tray.
Put the kale into the boiling water for 3 minutes to soften and then scoop
out and leave to cool.

Put the pan back on the heat and place the shallots in the water to simmer
for 10 minutes. Drain and leave to cool until they can be handled. Peel
away the outer skins and place the shallots into a shallow non-stick pan.
Sprinkle them with the soft brown sugar, balsamic vinegar and a drizzle of
rapeseed oil. Put on a low heat and cook until the sugar has melted and the
shallots have turned brown and sticky.

For the sauce

Pour the Port into a saucepan and heat until the liquid has reduced by half.
This will take 10 to 15 minutes. Add the stock or water, two thirds of the
blackberries, the vinegar, star anise and sugar then reduce again, this time
by two thirds. This will take around 15 minutes.

Pass the sauce through a sieve into another pan, stir in the cornflour paste,
season and simmer for a few minutes until the mixture thickens. Stir in the
butter and remaining blackberries.

To serve

When the duck legs are nearly ready, heat the remaining rapeseed oil (four
or five tablespoons) in a large non-stick pan and sauté your new potatoes
until golden. Stir in the kale and shallots and cook for another 2 minutes.

Remove the duck from the oven and arrange on plates with the kale,
shallots and potatoes. Drizzle the blackberry and Port sauce over the top.

Duck Cassoulet

If you already have some confit duck, then this is an easy, quick and hearty supper. If not, using roast duck leg is a tasty alternative and not much more effort.

Serves: 2 | Preparation time: 15 minutes | Cooking time: 1 hour 10 minutes

Ingredients

2 Gressingham duck legs

(or 2 confit duck legs)

1 tbsp olive oil

1 onion, peeled and diced

1 stick of celery, trimmed and quartered

1 carrot, peeled and diced

100g smoked bacon, cut into lardons

4 cloves of garlic, peeled and crushed

200ml chicken stock

(fresh or made from bouillon)

175ml white wine

1 tin of chopped tomatoes

1 tin of cannellini beans, drained

1 sprig of fresh thyme

1 bay leaf

Method

Preheat the oven to 200°c or 180°c fan. Dry the duck legs well with kitchen paper. Using a skewer or sharp knife, prick the skin all over and season well with salt and pepper. Transfer to a roasting tin and cook in the preheated oven for 30 minutes.

Heat the olive oil in an ovenproof saucepan or casserole dish on a low to medium heat. Add the onion, celery, carrot and bacon lardons. Gently cook for 5 minutes, then add the garlic and chicken stock. Continue to cook until the sauce starts to stick to the bottom of the pan. Pour in the wine to deglaze the pan and scrape up any sticky goodness.

Stir in the chopped tomatoes, cannellini beans, thyme and bay leaf. Bring to the boil and simmer gently for 15 minutes. Season to taste. When the duck legs have had 30 minutes, remove them from the oven, turning the temperature down to 180°c or 160°c fan, and carefully place them into the casserole dish on top of the sauce. If you are using confit duck, it can be added at this stage.

Place the casserole dish into the oven to finish cooking for 40 minutes. Place the cassoulet into the middle of the table to share and serve with plenty of crusty bread.

Duck Breast
with Redcurrant Jus

A classic midweek supper recipe.
I like to serve this with crispy rosemary and sea salt potatoes.

Serves: 4 | Preparation time: 10 minutes | Cooking time: 40 minutes

Ingredients

4 Gressingham duck breasts

200ml good red wine

1 tbsp redcurrant jelly (we prefer Stokes)

1 tsp balsamic vinegar

500ml chicken stock

Knob of unsalted butter

Method

Preheat your oven to 220°c or 200°c fan. Dry the duck breasts thoroughly with kitchen roll to remove excess moisture. Lightly score the skin six to eight times with a sharp knife then season.

Place the breasts skin side down in a cold non-stick ovenproof frying pan over a medium heat with no oil. Cook for 6 to 8 minutes or until golden brown, pouring off the fat regularly. When the skin is crisp, turn the duck breasts over and seal the other side for 30 seconds.

Transfer the pan to the middle of the preheated oven and cook the duck breasts for anywhere between 10 and 20 minutes, until the duck is done to your liking. Take them out the oven and rest somewhere warm for 10 minutes.

Once rested, transfer the duck breast to a board. Drain off any excess fat from the frying pan and place over a medium heat on the hob. Deglaze the pan with the red wine for a minute or two, scraping the bottom with a spatula. Add the redcurrant jelly and balsamic vinegar, then reduce until it starts to get sticky. Pour in the chicken stock and simmer until the liquid has reduced by three quarters. Whisk in a knob of butter then pour the sauce into a warm jug.

Carve each duck breast into six to eight slices, place onto warm plates and serve with your sauce and chosen vegetables. I like to serve this with rosemary and sea salt potatoes, buttered carrots and fried courgettes.

DISHES
FOR
SHARING

Country Duck Soup

A hearty winter warmer for a filling lunch or supper. Serve with crusty bread or just as it is;
the beans and potatoes make this soup a complete meal.

Serves: 6 | Preparation time: 20 minutes | Cooking time: 1 hour

Ingredients

4 tbsp olive oil

2 onions, peeled and chopped

2 sticks of celery, chopped into 1cm slices

4 carrots, peeled and sliced

4 medium potatoes, peeled and diced into 2cm cubes

1 small swede, peeled and diced into 2cm cubes

3 cloves of garlic, peeled and finely chopped

2 sprigs of thyme

2 tsp freshly ground black pepper

2 tbsp tomato purée

1.2 litres chicken stock

1 bay leaf

½ a medium savoy cabbage, roughly chopped

1 tin of cannellini beans, drained (400g)

400g cooked shredded Gressingham duck

Small bunch of flat leaf parsley, roughly chopped

Method

Heat the olive oil in a large lidded saucepan over a medium heat. Add the onion and celery, then cook gently for 5 minutes until the onions have softened.

Add the carrots, potatoes, swede, garlic and thyme to the pan. Season with salt and the black pepper, then cook gently for another 5 minutes, stirring occasionally.

Stir in the tomato purée and cook for a further 2 minutes before adding the stock and bay leaf. Cover with a lid and bring slowly to the boil. Reduce the heat to a simmer and cook for 20 minutes until the vegetables are tender.

Add the cabbage, cannellini beans and cooked shredded duck to the pan, then cook for a further 10 minutes. If the soup is too thick, add some hot water to reach your preferred consistency.

Finally, stir in the chopped flat leaf parsley, season to taste and serve with warm crusty bread.

Duck Croquettes

These make a lovely starter or light yet sophisticated evening meal served with a crisp green salad and garlic mayonnaise for dipping. Manchego is a Spanish sheep's milk cheese with a nutty flavour that complements the leek and melts well.

Makes: 12 | Preparation time: 30 minutes, plus 1 hour 30 minutes chilling | Cooking time: 50 minutes

Ingredients

100ml chicken stock

300ml full-fat milk

Pinch of freshly grated nutmeg

75ml extra-virgin olive oil

½ a leek, washed and finely chopped

150g plain flour

300g cooked shredded Gressingham duck, chilled

75g manchego, grated

1 tsp mustard powder

½ tsp paprika

2 large free-range eggs, beaten

75g panko breadcrumbs

200ml vegetable oil, for frying

2 cloves of garlic, finely chopped

4 heaped tbsp good quality mayonnaise

Method

To make the filling, first combine the stock, milk and nutmeg in a small pan. Bring to boiling point, then take off the heat. Put the olive oil in another saucepan on a low heat. Add the leek and sauté until soft, then stir in 75g of the flour and cook for 3 to 4 minutes until golden.

Gradually add the warm milk and stock to the flour mixture, being careful to whisk everything into a smooth paste each time before adding more liquid. Once all the liquid is incorporated, continue to cook the sauce over a medium heat for approximately 10 minutes until it thickens to the consistency of mashed potato.

Remove the pan from the heat and leave to cool for 10 minutes before adding the shredded duck, manchego, mustard and paprika. Season and mix well, then pour the mixture onto a lined 30 by 20cm baking tray and spread out flat. Cover with cling film and place in the fridge to chill for 1 hour.

Set out three bowls, one for the remaining flour, one for the beaten eggs and one for the breadcrumbs. Cut the chilled croquette mixture in half lengthways and then into six widthways so you have 12 sections. Roll each section into a barrel shape.

Dip each barrel first into the flour, then the eggs and then coat in the breadcrumbs. Place on a clean baking tray and repeat until they're all done. Chill the coated croquettes for 30 minutes.

When you are ready to cook the croquettes, preheat the oven to 200°c or 180°c fan. Put the vegetable oil into a heavy-bottomed pan on a medium heat. When the oil is hot, fry the croquettes on both sides until golden brown. Transfer them to a lined baking tray and finish cooking in the preheated oven for 10 minutes.

Stir the garlic into the mayonnaise, then serve it as a dip for the warm croquettes with a crisp green salad on the side.

Chilli con Canard

A delicious twist on the classic chilli con carne, using shredded cooked duck legs instead of beef. You can use kidney beans or black beans depending on your preference, and serve this with rice, tortilla chips or both.

Serves: 4 | Preparation time: 20 minutes | Cooking time: 60 minutes

Ingredients

2 large Gressingham duck legs

I red onion, peeled and finely sliced

Vegetable oil

2 cloves of garlic, peeled and crushed

100g cooking chorizo

2 tsp ground cumin

I tsp dried oregano

I tsp smoked paprika

I tbsp tomato purée

½ tbsp chipotle paste

I tin of kidney beans, drained (400g)

I tin of chopped tomatoes (400g)

I lime, halved

To serve

Fresh coriander

Soured cream

Grated cheese

Fresh chillies

Tortilla chips

Rice

Method

Preheat the oven to 200°c or 180°c fan. Pat the duck legs dry with kitchen towel. Prick the skin all over with a fork or sharp knife and season well with salt and pepper. Place them on a baking tray and into the preheated oven. Cook for 45 minutes then remove from the oven, leave until cool enough to handle and shred the meat from the bones with two forks.

Meanwhile, gently fry the red onion with a little oil in a pan over a low to medium heat until softened. Add the garlic and chorizo and cook for 3 to 4 minutes.

Next add the cumin, oregano, paprika, tomato purée, chipotle paste, kidney beans and chopped tomatoes. Turn up the heat and simmer for 10 minutes, then stir in the shredded duck and a little water if the sauce is getting too thick. Cook the chilli for a further 10 minutes, then finish with salt, pepper and lime juice to taste. Add a sprinkle of paprika if you like, then serve the chilli alongside all your chosen accompaniments.

Zesty Roast Spatchcock Poussin

This zesty roast spatchcock poussin recipe is perfect for summer, A dressed mixed salad and simple fries or crusty fresh bread will go well with this. Double up ingredients if cooking for more guests.

Serves: 2 | Preparation time: 10-15 minutes | Cooking time: 30-35 minutes

Ingredients

1 whole poussin

1 tbsp olive oil

50g softened butter

1 lemon

4 cloves of garlic, peeled and crushed

2-3 sprigs of thyme

2 tbsp dry white wine

1 tbsp mayonnaise

Pinch of paprika

Lemon wedges, to serve

Method

Preheat the oven to 200°c or 180°c fan. First, spatchcock the poussin. Place the poussin on a chopping board, breast side down. Using a sharp pair of scissors with the cavity facing you, cut close to each side of the back bone to remove it. Turn the poussin over and push down with your hand or the back of a large knife to flatten the bird.

Place the prepared poussin in a small roasting tray. Rub the olive oil all over the skin and season well with salt and pepper. Put the poussin breast side up and dot the butter on top.

Halve the lemon and cut four thin slices from the thickest part. Put two slices on top of the poussin and two underneath the bird along with the garlic. Add the thyme and the remaining lemon to the tray. Pour in the white wine.

Place the tray in the preheated oven and cook for 30 to 35 minutes. Baste after 15 minutes, and after 30 minutes check whether the bird is cooked by poking a skewer into the thickest part of the leg. If the juices run clear and the legs have loosened it's ready.

Place the mayonnaise in a ramekin and sprinkle the paprika over the top. Serve the poussin with the lemon wedges, mayonnaise and a fresh sprig of thyme to garnish.

By Paul Thompson at Paul Thompson Events

Canard Au Vin

This recipe is Gressingham's version of the French classic, coq au vin, which is made with chicken, but we like to use duck, of course! Red burgundy works well but any medium weight red wine will suffice. Best enjoyed with creamy mash and simple buttered greens.

Serves: 4 | Preparation time: 10 minutes | Cooking time: 1 hour 30 minutes

Ingredients

Sunflower or rapeseed oil

4 Gressingham duck legs

2 tbsp plain flour

50g unsalted butter

1 onion, peeled and finely sliced

1 carrot, peeled and diced into 1cm cubes

2 cloves of garlic, peeled and finely diced

200g chestnut mushrooms, sliced

100g smoked bacon lardons

750ml good red wine

Small bunch of fresh thyme

4 bay leaves

3 tsp cornflour (optional)

Method

Preheat the oven to 180°c or 160°c fan. Heat a casserole dish on the hob with a little oil over a high heat. Toss the duck legs in the flour, knocking off any excess, then fry on either side in the pan until golden brown. Season and remove from the pan to rest somewhere warm.

Melt the butter in the casserole dish then add the onion, carrot, garlic, mushrooms and bacon. Fry for 3 to 4 minutes while scraping the bottom of the pan with a wooden spatula, to make sure nothing sticks and burns.

Pour in the red wine then add the herbs and duck legs. Bring to the boil and season. Place a lid on the casserole dish then transfer to the oven and cook for 1 hour 20 minutes.

When the cooking time is up, remove the casserole from the oven. Skim off and discard any excess fat from the surface, then gently stir the canard au vin and taste the sauce to adjust the seasoning if needed. Traditionally, the dish is now served from the casserole at the table.

However, if you prefer a richer gravy, strain the liquid from the casserole into a saucepan over a low to medium heat. Simmer while you make a paste (called a slurry) with the cornflour and a little cold water, then whisk this into the sauce until you have the consistency you prefer. Return the sauce to the casserole dish and stir well before serving.

Vietnamese Table Salad with Roast Poussin

This sharing dish is popular, easy to pull together and healthy. We've used roast poussin but it's equally delicious with duck, chicken or fish. You can also mix and match other salad ingredients.

Serves: 4 | Preparation time: 30 minutes | Cooking time: 45 minutes

Ingredients

2 whole poussins

1 chilli, finely chopped

2 tsp peeled and finely chopped root ginger

1 lime, juiced

1 clove of garlic, peeled and finely chopped

1 tsp soft brown sugar

1 tbsp light olive oil

For the salad

2 gem lettuces, leaves separated and washed

2 medium carrots, peeled and grated

2 red chillies, thinly sliced

2 spring onions, thinly sliced

2 limes, cut into wedges

100g rice vermicelli noodles, cooked

Small bunch of fresh mint

Small bunch of fresh coriander

Rice paper pancakes (optional)

Method

Preheat the oven to 200°c or 180°c fan. Combine the chilli, ginger, lime juice, garlic, sugar and light olive oil in a bowl then mix well.

Pat the poussin dry with paper towels. Season well with salt and pepper inside and out then place the birds into a roasting tray. Spread the chilli and ginger marinade all over the birds and then put them in the preheated oven to roast for 45 minutes.

Meanwhile, prepare the salad ingredients and lay everything out in the middle of your table. The idea is to have everything in little bowls so people can pick and choose what to include. Sweet chilli sauce is also a good accompaniment here.

Once you have roasted your birds, remove from the oven and allow them to rest for 15 minutes. Take them to the table and shred the meat off with two forks.

When everything is ready to eat, you can each take a pancake or a lettuce leaf, pile it up with a mixture of salad, herbs, noodles, lime juice, chillies and shredded poussin then tuck in.

By Chris Connell and Jess Celyn, Gressingham customers

Duck Paella

This dish combines a classic tapas dish with a delicious paella. You can leave the paella to catch on the base of the pan to make a crisp crust at the bottom; this is called 'socarrat' and much fought over...it's the best bit!

Serves: 4 as a starter, 2 as a main | Preparation time: 10 minutes | Cooking time: 45-50 minutes

Ingredients

½ a chorizo ring, cut into thin semi-circles

Good olive oil

3-4 Gressingham duck breasts, skin scored

100ml good Spanish Rioja or other red wine

1 tbsp runny honey

1 red onion, peeled and chopped

2 sweet peppers, deseeded and cut into small large dice

2 cloves of garlic, peeled and crushed

800ml good stock (preferably beef)

1 tsp sweet paprika

½ tsp turmeric

½ tsp ground ginger

Small pinch of saffron strands

250ml paella rice (such as bomba or Calasparra)

Method

In a large, deep sauté pan on a medium-high heat, fry the chorizo in a good glug of oil until the oil starts to turn red. Make a space in the pan to lay in the duck breasts skin side down and then turn down the heat to low-medium. Fry for 5 to 8 minutes until the skin is crisping up. Turn the breasts over and cook on all sides until browned. Remove the duck and chorizo with a slotted spoon and place them in a hot dish to keep warm.

Pour the wine into the pan and turn up the heat, boiling to reduce the liquid to a thin syrupy consistency. Add the honey and mix well. Return the duck to the pan, skin side up, along with the chorizo and cook over a low-medium heat for 10 minutes or so, basting regularly. Transfer the duck back to the hot dish and keep warm.

Add the onions, peppers and garlic to the chorizo and cook over a medium-high heat for 5 to 10 minutes while you prepare the cooking liquor. Bring 700ml of the stock to a simmer with the spices in a saucepan. Next stir the rice into the paella pan. Pour in the spiced stock, bring back to a boil over a high heat and cook vigorously for 5 minutes while stirring regularly.

Turn the heat down low and cook for about 10 to 12 minutes until the rice is tender. Do not stir the rice while cooking, but if it looks like it is getting dry at the bottom of the pan and you don't want a crispy crust, just add a little of the remaining hot stock. Return the sliced duck to the paella just before serving.

By Pascal Pommier, The Table

Parmentier de Canard (Duck 'Shepherd's Pie')

A delicious, simple midweek supper dish, perfect at the end of a hard winter's day of walking or working! Best enjoyed simply with buttered garden peas or perhaps a dressed leaf salad, such as lamb's lettuce and rocket.

Serves: 6 | Preparation time: 5 minutes | Cooking time: 40 minutes

Ingredients

1kg fluffy potatoes for mashing

6 Gressingham confit duck legs

200ml full-fat milk

25g unsalted butter, softened

150g mature cheddar, grated

Method

Preheat the oven to 200°c or 180°c fan. Peel and cut the potatoes into a large dice. Simmer in a large pan of salted water and cook until tender, about 15 to 20 minutes. Drain well and place back in the saucepan on the turned-off hob to steam dry for a few minutes.

While the potatoes are cooking, place the confit duck legs in a deep frying pan and heat up gently for 15 minutes over a low-medium heat.

Heat the milk with the butter until steaming. Mash the potatoes well or push through a potato ricer. Stir the hot buttery milk into the potatoes and season to taste. Cover and keep warm.

Using two forks, remove the meat from the duck legs and shred into pieces. Add the meat to a wide gratin dish. Top the duck with the mash before sprinkling over the cheese. Bake for 20 minutes until browned on top. Carefully remove the pie from the oven and serve.

Puff Pastry
Duck Pie

This is comfort food at its best. Serve with seasonal greens
and creamy mashed potato if you like.

Serves: 6 | Preparation time: 30 minutes | Cooking time: 2 hours

Ingredients

4 Gressingham duck legs

4 rashers of smoked bacon, diced

3 cloves of garlic, peeled and finely chopped

I onion, peeled and diced

I tbsp tomato purée

3 sprigs of thyme

500ml good red wine

300ml chicken stock

I large carrot, peeled and diced

I leek, washed and sliced

I tbsp cornflour

I packet of ready-rolled puff pastry (320g)

I egg, beaten

Method

Prepare the duck legs by removing any excess fat, piercing the skin all over with a skewer and seasoning well. Place a casserole dish on a medium heat and sear the duck legs gently skin side down until the fat has rendered. Turn the legs over and sear the other side until golden brown, then remove the duck from the pan.

Carefully pour off the excess duck fat from the pan. Add the bacon, garlic and onion then fry gently for 5 minutes, or until the onion has softened. Add the tomato purée and thyme, cook for a further 2 minutes, then place the duck legs back in the pan. Cover them with the wine and stock, then leave to simmer for I hour with the lid on.

After the hour, add the carrot and leek to the pan. Cook for a further 30 minutes, then carefully lift the duck legs out of the pan, remove the meat from the bone and set aside in a warm place. Mix the cornflour with two tablespoons of cold water and add the paste to the pan, stirring until the mixture thickens and turns glossy. Fold the duck meat back into the sauce, taste to check the seasoning, then spoon your pie filling into six individual dishes and allow to cool.

Unroll and cut out pieces of pastry large enough to top each pie. Brush the edge of each dish with a little beaten egg. Place the pastry on top and press firmly on the edges. Trim off any excess pastry with a sharp knife, then brush the pie lids with beaten egg. You can store the pies in the fridge for up to three days at this point. When you are ready to cook, place the pies in a preheated oven at 180°c for 35 minutes until the pastry is risen and golden.

Middle Eastern Shredded Duck Wraps

This sort of meal is great for bringing everyone to the table and letting them customise flavours and textures. The spice blend ras el hanout, whose name simply means 'top shelf' in Arabic, is found in varying forms across North Africa, but is sold in supermarkets and online.

Serves: 4 | Preparation time: 30 minutes, plus marinating | Cooking time: 1 hour 30 minutes

Ingredients

½ tsp ground ginger

1 tsp ground cinnamon

1 tsp ras el hanout

1 tbsp runny honey

2 tbsp rapeseed oil

1 tsp orange flower water (optional)

2 Gressingham duck legs

For the hummus

400g tin of chickpeas, drained

100ml olive oil

1-2 cloves of garlic, peeled and crushed

1 lemon, juiced

2 tbsp tahini

1 tsp ground cumin

For the cucumber and yoghurt salad

1 cucumber

1 clove of garlic, finely chopped

½ a lemon, juiced

200g full-fat Greek yoghurt

Handful of mint leaves, chopped

To serve

8 flatbreads or tortilla wraps

1 packet of washed mixed leaves

Method

In a small bowl, mix the ginger, cinnamon and ras el hanout with the honey, rapeseed oil and orange flower water if using. Rub this paste into the duck legs then leave to marinate for a minimum of 1 hour and preferably overnight. When you are ready to cook, preheat the oven to 160°c or 140°c fan.

Place the marinated duck legs on a baking tray, pierce the skin all over with a skewer and season on both sides. Cook in the preheated oven for 1 hour 30 minutes, until the skin is crispy and the meat falls away from the bone.

Meanwhile, prepare your accompaniments. Place all the ingredients for the hummus into a food processor and blitz until smooth. Adding a tablespoon or two of boiling water during the blending will help to achieve a smooth, silky finish. Season to taste.

Halve the cucumber lengthways then use a teaspoon to scrape out the seeds and watery centre. Thinly slice into half-moons, then add the cucumber to a bowl with the garlic, lemon juice, yoghurt and chopped mint (keeping a pinch back for garnish). Mix and season to taste.

Once the duck has cooked, shred the meat off the bones using two forks. Place into a bowl and spoon over the cooking juices. Taste to check the seasoning, then cover to keep warm.

When you're ready to serve up, heat the flatbreads in a dry frying pan or on a chargrill. Place the warm shredded duck, hummus and salads on the table then let your guests build their own wraps and tuck in.

By Rebecca Alderton

Slow Cooker Red Thai Duck and Sweet Potato Curry

A simple supper idea for busy weeknights by Gressingham employee Rebecca Alderton, who loves using her slow cooker to create tasty meals for her family.

Serves: 4 | Preparation time: 10 minutes | Cooking time: 4-6 hours

Ingredients

3 or 4 Gressingham duck legs

300g sweet potatoes

3 carrots

1 onion

2.5cm fresh ginger

1 bulb of garlic

1 tsp salt

1 tbsp sugar

1 tbsp fish sauce

1 tbsp ground cumin

2 tbsp red Thai curry paste

1 tin of coconut milk

1 chicken stock cube

400ml water

Method

First, prepare the vegetables. Peel and chop the sweet potatoes, carrots, onion, ginger and garlic. Meanwhile, warm up the slow cooker if necessary.

Place all of the ingredients in the slow cooker and cook on high for 4 hours, or low for 6 hours. Stir occasionally while cooking.

When the duck legs are cooked, remove them from the cooker and discard the fat then shred the meat using two forks. Stir the shredded duck back into the vegetables and sauce.

Serve the curry with turmeric rice.

REMARKABLE
ROASTS

Summer Roast Duck Crown

A very easy cut of duck to roast and carve for an informal summer lunch, served with potato wedges, salad and a lovely citrus and herb mayonnaise.

Serves: 4 | Preparation time: 10 minutes, plus 10 minutes resting | Cooking time: 1 hour

Ingredients

2 tbsp vegetable oil or duck fat

500g Maris Piper potatoes, washed and cut into wedges (skins on)

2-3 sprigs of rosemary

2-3 sprigs of thyme

1 Gressingham duck crown (approx. 1kg)

200g good quality mayonnaise

½ a lemon, zested and juiced

Small bunch of flat leaf parsley, washed and chopped

Small handful of seedless grapes, halved

200g mixed leaves, washed

300g cherry tomatoes on the vine

Method

Preheat the oven to 200°c or 180°c fan. Put the vegetable oil or duck fat into a roasting tin and place in the oven for 10 minutes to heat up. Carefully tip the potatoes, rosemary and thyme into the tin, gently stir the potatoes to coat them then season well with salt and pepper.

Prepare the duck by drying the crown with kitchen towel and then seasoning inside and out with salt and pepper. Place the crown in the middle of the roasting tin surrounded by the potato wedges. Roast for 40 to 50 minutes until the skin of the duck is crisp and golden.

While your duck is cooking, combine the mayonnaise with the lemon zest, lemon juice and chopped parsley then season to taste. Toss the grapes and mixed leaves together with a squeeze of lemon juice.

Carefully remove the roasting tin from the oven and rest the duck crown somewhere warm for at least 10 minutes before serving. Place the vine tomatoes on top of the wedges and return them to the oven for 10 minutes.

Carve the duck on a warm platter and serve alongside the wedges, roasted vine tomatoes, mayonnaise and plenty of warm crusty bread.

Glazed Cardamom and Honey Whole Roast Duck

A trusty recipe for this traditional Sunday favourite. Nothing beats a perfect Gressingham duck with all of the trimmings! Remember to save the duck fat for making delicious crispy roast potatoes.

Serves: 4 | Preparation time: 10 minutes. plus 30-45 minutes resting | Cooking time: 2 hours (weight dependent)

Ingredients

1 whole Gressingham duck (approx. 2.2kg)

½ a bulb of garlic, halved horizontally

For the glaze

3 tbsp runny honey

1 tbsp dry sherry

1 tsp cracked black pepper

1 orange, zested and juiced

5 cardamom pods, husks removed and seeds crushed

For the potatoes and sauce

1kg new potatoes, halved lengthways

½ tsp turmeric

Knob of butter

1 tsp cumin seeds

2 tbsp rapeseed oil

Method

Preheat the oven to 200°c or 180°c fan. Remove all the packaging from the duck along with the bag of giblets (if included). Weigh the duck to calculate the roasting time. It will need 20 minutes per 500g plus an additional 20 minutes.

Pat the duck skin dry with a kitchen towel. Prick the skin in and around the point where the thigh meets the breast. Season well with salt and pepper inside and out and place the garlic inside the cavity. Put the duck on a rack within a roasting tin and place in the preheated oven to roast.

Cook the potatoes for 20 minutes in boiling salted water with the turmeric. Meanwhile, prepare the glaze by mixing the honey, sherry, pepper, orange zest, orange juice and crushed cardamom seeds together in a small pan. Gently heat until combined and keep warm.

10 minutes before the end of the cooking time, brush the duck with the warm glaze and return to the oven to finish roasting. Remove the duck once cooked and carefully transfer to a warm plate. Leave it to rest for approximately 30 minutes while you finish the accompaniments.

Spoon off any excess fat from the roasting tin and add 200ml of hot water to the remaining juices. Bring the sauce to the boil, whisk in the knob of butter, set aside and keep warm.

Place a frying pan on a medium heat, add the cumin seeds and carefully dry fry for 2 to 3 minutes. Add the rapeseed oil to the pan before adding the boiled and drained potatoes. Sauté for 2 to 3 minutes then season with salt and pepper to taste.

Carve the rested duck and serve with the sauce, potatoes and your choice of greens.

Whole Roast Duck with Honey and Rosemary

This is a real Gressingham favourite, perfect for a smart dinner party or Sunday lunch. Delicious served with duck fat roast potatoes and all the trimmings.

Serves: 4 | Preparation time: 15 minutes, plus 35-40 minutes resting | Cooking time: 2 hours (weight dependent)

Ingredients

1 whole Gressingham duck (approx. 2.2kg)

1kg roasting potatoes

4 tbsp Gressingham duck fat

4 sprigs of fresh rosemary

1 onion, roughly chopped

2 bulbs of garlic, halved horizontally

250ml good dry white wine

400ml chicken stock

3 tbsp runny honey

50g butter

Method

Preheat the oven to 200°c or 180°c fan. Weigh the duck to calculate the roasting time. It will need 20 minutes per 500g plus an additional 20 minutes. Pat the skin dry with a kitchen towel. Pick the skin in and around the point where the thigh meets the breast. Season well with salt and pepper inside and out, then place the duck on a rack within a large roasting tin.

Place the duck in the preheated oven to cook for the calculated time. While your duck is roasting, prepare your potatoes. Peel and chop them into large chunks, then cook in boiling salted water until just tender. Drain and let them steam dry off the heat.

When the duck has been roasting for 45 minutes, add the duck fat to the tin and return it to the oven for 5 minutes to heat the fat. Add the potatoes, rosemary, onion and garlic to the tin. Lightly season with salt and place back in the oven for the remaining duck cooking time.

When the duck is done, remove it from the tin and leave it to rest for 30 to 45 minutes somewhere warm. Baste the potatoes in the fat and return them to the oven while the duck is resting. When done, transfer the roast potatoes to a hot platter and carefully pour off any excess fat from the tin. You should be left with just the juices, rosemary, onion and garlic.

Add the wine to the tin, place it on the hob and bring to the boil, scraping off anything stuck to the bottom with a wooden spatula. Simmer for 5 minutes, then pass the gravy through a fine sieve into a saucepan. Add the hot chicken stock to the saucepan and boil until the liquid has reduced by half and thickened to a gravy consistency. Stir in the honey and check the sauce for seasoning and sweetness, then stir in the butter.

Carve the duck onto warm plates and serve with the roast potatoes, sauce and trimmings.

Roast Guinea Fowl

Often described as 'how chicken used to taste' guinea fowl is a traditional bird, simple to cook for a succulent white meat with a subtle gamey taste.

Serves: 2-3 | Preparation time: 5 minutes, plus 10-20 minutes resting | Cooking time: 1 hour 5 minutes

Ingredients

1 Gressingham guinea fowl

Sunflower or good rapeseed oil

Salt and black pepper

Method

Preheat your oven to 190°c or 170°c fan. Remove all the packaging, put the bird in a roasting tin and brush with oil. Season the bird well with salt and pepper inside and out.

Place on the middle shelf of the oven and roast for 1 hour 5 minutes. Make sure the meat is hot and the leg bones have loosened. Insert a skewer into the thickest part of the leg to see if the juices run clear. If they do, the guinea fowl is cooked.

When done, remove the guinea fowl from the oven, cover loosely with foil and rest for 10 to 20 minutes before carving.

Traditional Roast Goose

There's nothing more traditional for Christmas Day than the splendid centrepiece of a whole roast goose, but of course it is delicious any time of year. Remember that cooking appliances can vary in performance so these are guidelines, but you can't go wrong with this easy recipe.

Serves: 8 | Preparation time: 15 minutes, plus 30 minutes resting | Cooking time: 2-2½ hours

Ingredients

4-5kg Gressingham goose

2 large carrots

2 sticks of celery

4 red onions, halved

4 cloves of garlic

Sprig of rosemary

Vegetable oil

Sea salt

Method

Preheat your oven to 180°c or 160°c fan. Remove the giblets and any spare fat from inside the cavity of the goose, then weigh the bird to calculate the cooking time. It will need 30 minutes per kilogram.

Take a large roasting tin and make a bed for your goose using the carrots, celery and three of the onions. Place the goose on the vegetables and prick the skin all over with a fork or cocktail stick, particularly around the legs and wings. Season the inside of the goose and place the garlic, rosemary and remaining two onion halves inside the cavity. Rub the skin all over with a little oil and season generously with salt.

Cover the tin loosely with foil and place in the middle of the preheated oven. Baste the goose twice during its cooking time with the juices and fat that will collect in the tin. Remove the foil for the last 30 minutes of roasting time. Once cooked, lift the goose onto a warm carving platter and loosely cover it with the foil. Leave to rest for 30 minutes before carving and serving.

Festive Roast Turkey

To get the best out of this Christmas favourite, follow our simple step-by-step guide on how to cook a traditional roast turkey without any fuss. Cooking appliances do vary in performance, so these are our guidelines.

Serves: 8 | Preparation time: 15 minutes, plus 30-45 minutes resting | Cooking time: 2 hours 20 minutes - 2 hours 40 minutes

Ingredients

4-5kg Gressingham turkey

200g unsalted butter, softened

2 sprigs of thyme

2 bay leaves

Salt and black pepper

Method

Remove the turkey from the refrigerator 2 hours prior to cooking. Remove all the packaging and take out the giblet bag (save this for making stock). Pat the skin dry with a kitchen towel. Preheat the oven to 200°c or 180°c fan.

To calculate the cooking time, check the weight label or weigh your turkey. Allow 20 minutes per kilogram plus an additional 70 minutes.

Place the turkey into a deep roasting tin. Rub half of the butter over the skin, placing the remainder inside the bird with the thyme and bay leaves. Season well inside and out with salt and pepper. Add 500ml of water to the tray around the bird.

Cover the turkey loosely with foil, making sure it is well sealed around the edges of the tin. Place in the preheated oven and cook for 45 minutes, then reduce the temperature to 160°c or 140°c fan. After 1 hour at this temperature, remove the foil and cook the turkey uncovered for the remaining cooking time.

To check whether the turkey is done, insert a skewer or knife into the point where the thigh meets the breast. The juices should run clear, so if they are not clear return the turkey to the oven for a further 20 minutes then check again. Alternatively, check with a digital meat thermometer for a temperature of 70°c which indicates the turkey is safely cooked.

Transfer the bird to a warm platter, cover loosely with foil and allow to rest for 30 to 45 minutes before carving. Reserve the cooking juices to make your gravy. Serve with all the trimmings.

Duck Fat
Roast Potatoes

The fat from your roast duck makes perfect crispy roast potatoes. Ideal for Sunday lunch or
Christmas dinner.

Serves: 4 | Preparation time: 5 minutes | Cooking time: 1 hour

Ingredients

1.5kg large Maris Piper potatoes, peeled and
cut into a good eating size

1 tsp salt

6 tbsp duck fat or good vegetable oil

Pinch of white pepper

3 sprigs of rosemary

3 cloves of garlic, crushed

Method

Preheat the oven to 200°c or 180°c fan. Cover the potatoes with cold water in a large saucepan and add the salt. Bring to the boil then simmer for a further 10 minutes. turn off the heat, drain the potatoes well, return them to the pan and allow them to steam for a few minutes off the heat.

Meanwhile, decant the duck fat (or oil) into a large deep sided roasting tray and place in the oven to heat. After 5 minutes or so, remove the tray from the oven and carefully place the potatoes into the hot fat. Lightly season with salt and white pepper. Add the rosemary and garlic then return the tray to the oven.

Cook for 35 to 45 minutes until the potatoes are crisp and golden. Remove the tin from the oven, carefully drain off the fat (saving it for next time) and serve.

Apple Sauce

Serves: 6-8 | Preparation time: 10 minutes | Cooking time: 20 minutes

Ingredients

500g cooking apples (such as Bramleys)

1 lemon, zested and juiced

3 tbsp water

1 tbsp sugar

Knob of butter

Method

Peel core, and roughly chop the apples then put them into a saucepan with the lemon zest, half the juice, all the water and the sugar. Place on a low heat and cook gently until the apples are soft and all the liquid has been absorbed. Beat the butter into the sauce with a wooden spoon. Taste and add a little sugar if required. Can be served hot or cold.

Cranberry Sauce

Serves: 6-8 | Preparation time: 5 minutes | Cooking time: 20 minutes

Ingredients

100g light muscovado sugar

100ml orange juice

300g fresh or frozen cranberries

1 stick of cinnamon

1 star anise

Glug of Port

Method

Place the sugar and orange juice in a pan, heat gently until the sugar dissolves then add the cranberries. Bring back to the boil then reduce the heat to a simmer. Add the spices and Port to the pan and simmer until the cranberries soften. This will take between 5 and 10 minutes, depending on whether you are using frozen or fresh cranberries. Leave the sauce to cool, then serve at room temperature.

Bread Sauce

Serves: 6-8 | Preparation time: 10 minutes | Cooking time: 30 minutes

Ingredients

1 onion, peeled and left whole

6 whole cloves

575ml whole milk

1 bay leaf

8 black peppercorns

100g freshly made white breadcrumbs

50g butter

Pinch of freshly grated nutmeg

50ml double cream (optional)

Method

Stud the onion with the cloves and place in a saucepan with the milk, bay leaf and peppercorns. Bring the milk to just below boiling point then reduce the heat and simmer for 20 minutes. Strain the milk through a fine sieve then return it to the pan. Add the breadcrumbs and simmer for 3 to 4 minutes. Stir in the butter and nutmeg, season to taste then serve warm. For a more luxurious sauce, you can also fold in 50ml of double cream to finish.

Vichy Carrots

Serves: 6-8 | Preparation time: 10 minutes | Cooking time: 15 minutes

Ingredients

24 baby carrots, trimmed (or 6 large carrots, peeled and cut diagonally into 2cm slices)

50g butter

200ml water

1 tbsp caster sugar

½ a lemon, juiced

Small bunch of curly parsley, finely chopped

Method

Place all the ingredients except the parsley into a pan along with a good pinch of salt. Bring to the boil, reduce to a gentle simmer and cover with a lid. Simmer gently for 4 to 5 minutes until the carrots have softened but are still firm. Remove the lid, sprinkle with the parsley and lightly season before serving.

Roast Parsnips

Serves: 6-8 | Preparation time: 20 minutes | Cooking time: 45 minutes

Ingredients

2kg small parsnips, scrubbed and halved lengthways

200ml apple juice

Small bunch of fresh thyme

2 tbsp vegetable oil

2 tbsp runny honey

1 tbsp butter

Method

Preheat the oven to 190°c or 170°c fan. Place the parsnips into a pan on a medium heat with the apple juice and half the thyme. Season with salt and black pepper, bring to the boil and simmer for 5 to 7 minutes, then drain and set aside. Place the oil in a shallow roasting tray and preheat in the oven until smoking hot. Meanwhile, put the parsnips into a bowl with the honey and remaining thyme. Season again and mix well. Carefully tip the parsnips into the hot oil and roast for 40 minutes, turning once during cooking. Stir the butter into the roast parsnips before serving.

Pork and Apple Stuffing

Serves: 6-8 | Preparation time: 20 minutes | Cooking time: 45 minutes

Ingredients

50g butter

1 large onion, finely chopped

50g smoked pancetta cubes

450g good quality sausage meat

150g fresh white breadcrumbs

2 eating apples, peeled, cored and finely diced

Handful of fresh sage leaves, finely chopped

1 tsp dried mixed herbs

Method

Melt the butter in a frying pan over a medium heat. Add the onion and the pancetta to the pan, then fry gently for 10 minutes until the onion has softened and is light golden. Drain off any excess fat and leave to cool. Place the onions and pancetta into a large bowl with all the remaining ingredients. Season and mix well. Roll the stuffing into golf ball sized portions, place on a baking tray and leave to set in the fridge for 1 hour (this helps the balls to hold their shape when cooked). Bake for 30 minutes in a preheated oven at 190°c or 170°c fan until golden.

DISHES
FOR
ENTERTAINING

By Pascal Pommier, The Table

Confit de Canard à la Salardaise

This classic peasant dish comes from south-western France and is best enjoyed with a dressed green salad on the side.

Serves: 4 | Preparation time: 5 minutes | Cooking time: 50 minutes

Ingredients

4 Gressingham duck legs

3 cloves of garlic, peeled

4 sprigs of thyme

300g Gressingham duck fat

1kg good waxy potatoes

Small bunch of curly parsley

Method

Preheat the oven to 160°c or 140°c fan. Season the duck legs with salt and pepper, then place them skin side down in a heavy ovenproof earthenware pan or hob proof casserole (such as Le Creuset) with one of the garlic cloves and all the thyme.

Cover the legs with most of the duck fat, put on the lid and bring to a simmer over a low-medium heat. Transfer to the preheated oven and cook for 45 minutes.

Meanwhile, peel the potatoes and slice them into rounds. Thinly slice the remaining cloves of garlic and finely shred the parsley.

Fry the potatoes in the remaining duck fat in a deep sauté pan over a medium heat for about 10 minutes, until they are starting to brown. Remove any excess fat then stir in the garlic and parsley. Turn the heat down low and continue frying for another 15 minutes.

Remove the duck legs from the oven when they are done. Gently transfer them into another sauté pan over a medium-high heat and fry them on both sides until crispy. Serve the duck legs with the potatoes and a fresh green salad on the side. Enjoy!

Piri Piri Spatchcock Poussin and Cumin Potatoes

Perfect for al fresco dining, this can be finished off on the barbecue in the summer or, for a chargrilled finish, place the poussin onto a smoking griddle pan after roasting. It eats well with a dressed salad or seasonal vegetables.

Serves: 4 | Preparation time: 10 minutes | Cooking time: 1 hour 30 minutes

Ingredients

2 or 4 poussins

Salt and pepper

1 tbsp smoked paprika

2 cloves of garlic

2 red chillies, finely sliced

1 tbsp white wine vinegar

4 tbsp good rapeseed oil

1 tsp caster sugar

1 lemon, zested and juiced

500g new potatoes

125g duck fat

¼ tsp cumin seeds

Method

Preheat the oven to 180°c or 160°c fan. Prepare the poussins by placing them breast side down on a chopping board. Using a strong pair of scissors, cut down either side of the backbone from neck to tail. Remove the backbone and save for stock. Gently prize apart and push down on the breastbone to flatten. Turn the poussins over so the breasts are facing upwards. If you are unable to spatchcock the birds (it can be tricky if you do not have sharp scissors) then just roast them whole and joint them once cooked.

Prick the skin around the legs and season the birds on both sides with salt, pepper and half of the paprika. Place them on a baking tray, breast side up, and roast for 45 minutes in the preheated oven.

Meanwhile, start the piri piri sauce and the potatoes. Place the remaining paprika, garlic, chilli, vinegar, oil, sugar, lemon zest and lemon juice into a blender. Blitz until combined then use this marinade to baste the poussins five or six times while they cook.

In saucepan of boiling salted water, simmer the potatoes for 10 minutes until just softened. Put the duck fat in a deep sided baking tray. Place the tray into the oven and after 10 minutes, once the fat is hot, take the tray out carefully and add your potatoes, tossing them with the cumin seeds and some seasoning. Return to the oven for 20 to 30 minutes until golden.

When the poussins are cooked, remove from the oven and leave in a warm place to rest for a few minutes after basting once more with the marinade in the tray. Joint the poussins if you haven't spatchcocked them and serve on warm plates with the potatoes.

Honey and Marmalade Duck Legs with Sweet Potato Mash

A twist on the old favourite, duck à l'orange, thanks to the addition of a marmalade syrup which makes this dish sublime. Cook the legs until the meat is melt-in-the-mouth tender. A real treat ready in less than two hours. I serve this with simple green beans for contrast.

Serves: 2 | Preparation time: 10 minutes | Cooking time: 1 hour 30 minutes

Ingredients

2 Gressingham duck legs

1 tbsp runny honey

50g good marmalade

1 tbsp Cointreau (or other orange liqueur)

1 tbsp orange juice

200g sweet potatoes

A good knob of butter

½ tsp ground nutmeg

Handful of fresh coriander, chopped

Method

Preheat the oven to 180°c or 160°c fan. Pierce the skin on the duck legs all over with a fork or cocktail stick and season on both sides. Place the duck legs on a baking tray and roast in the preheated oven for about 1 hour 30 minutes. The meat should be very soft and the bones should pull away easily when they are done.

Start the syrup after an hour of roasting. Place the honey, marmalade, Cointreau and orange juice in a pan over a moderate heat to reduce until you have a sticky syrup. If it's too thick, stir in another splash of orange juice. Set aside until required.

Meanwhile, peel the sweet potatoes and cut them into 2cm dice. Steam or simmer the sweet potatoes until tender, then mash them with the butter and nutmeg. Season well to taste then fold in the coriander.

Slightly warm the syrup, place a scoop of mash on each plate, arrange a duck leg on top of it and spoon over the syrup to serve.

Tea-Smoked Duck Breast Salad

You will need a well ventilated room to make this in, as it can get quite smoky. It's worthwhile for the beautiful, subtle layers of flavour though, and can be kept in the fridge for up to three days before use. Great for a dinner party if made in advance!

Serves: 4 as a starter | Preparation time: 30 minutes | Cooking time: 30 minutes

Ingredients

For the smoked duck

200g uncooked rice

100g loose black tea leaves

4 star anise

3 sticks of cinnamon, broken in half

2 cloves of garlic, crushed

2cm root ginger, halved and flattened

1 tsp black peppercorns

1 chilli, halved lengthways

2 Gressingham duck breasts

For the salad

½ cucumber, peeled into ribbons

4 radishes, washed and finely sliced

4 gem lettuce leaves, sliced

1 tsp sushi ginger (optional)

Method

Line a wok with two layers of tin foil. Evenly spread out all the smoking ingredients in the base, then put the wok on a low heat and place a wire rack inside it over the smoking ingredients.

Dry the duck breasts well with kitchen paper. Lay them skin side down into an unoiled frying pan on a low to medium heat. Lightly season the meat. Cook for about 4 minutes or until the skin starts to crisp up. Transfer the duck breasts to the wire rack in the wok, laying them skin side up. Place a lid over the top, or cover with more foil, to keep the smoke in and turn the heat up to medium. Leave the duck to smoke for 10 minutes, then take the wok off the heat but leave it covered with the duck inside for another 10 minutes.

Arrange the salad ingredients neatly on one half of the plate. Carve the smoked duck into thin slices and lay them on the other half of the plate to serve.

By Lisa Sare, cook and food stylist

Fried Pheasant Breast with Pancetta and Sage

Local wild game is a delight in season. This eats well with creamed celeriac, braised savoy cabbage and roast parsnips.

Serves: 6-8 | Preparation time: 10 minutes | Cooking time: 10 minutes

Ingredients

4 pheasant breasts

Good rapeseed oil

Salt and black pepper

16 large sage leaves

1 pack of pancetta rashers

(very thin smoked streaky bacon would work well as an alternative)

Method

Place the pheasant breasts on a board, then lightly oil and season them well. Press four sage leaves evenly along the top of each breast.

Take out the thin slices of pancetta and carefully wrap around the pheasant breasts and sage, starting at one end until you have covered each one in turn. You may only need two slices for each, depending on the size of the breasts and rashers.

Heat up a non-stick oiled pan on a medium heat. Add the breasts sage-side down and sauté for about 5 minutes. Turn over and fry for another 5 minutes or until cooked. Rest the pheasant for 5 minutes before carving and serving with your choice of accompaniments.

Roast Duck Breast with Balsamic Glazed Root Vegetables

A warming autumnal dish with root vegetables and a sweet balsamic glaze. You could use other vegetables such as swede, parsnip, celeriac or sweet potato depending on the time of year.

Serves: 2 | Preparation time: 5 minutes | Cooking time: 45 minutes

Ingredients

2 Gressingham duck breasts

1 red onion, peeled and cut in quarters

1 large beetroot, peeled and cut into 2cm chunks

1 large carrot, peeled and cut into 2 cm chunks

1 large potato, peeled and cut into 2cm chunks

1 bulb of garlic, cut in horizontally

Few sprigs of rosemary and thyme

4 tbsp olive oil

2 tbsp balsamic glaze

Handful of spinach leaves, washed

Method

Preheat the oven to 200°c or 80°c fan. Put the onion, root vegetables, garlic and herbs into a roasting tray, drizzle with oil and season before mixing well. Place into the oven to roast for about 40 to 50 minutes, stirring once halfway through cooking.

When the vegetables have been in the oven for 20 minutes, start the Gressingham duck breasts. Place an empty baking tray into the oven below the veg to keep it warm.

Dry the duck breasts well with kitchen roll and lightly score the skin. Place the breasts skin side down in a frying pan on a medium heat with no oil. Cook for 6 to 8 minutes until the skin is golden and crispy. Carefully pour off any excess fat into a bowl as the duck is cooking. Once the skin is crispy, turn the duck over and sear the meat for 30 seconds.

Transfer the duck breasts to the heated baking tray and roast in the oven for 12 minutes, or longer if you like your duck well cooked. Remove from the oven and allow it to rest somewhere warm until the vegetables are cooked.

To finish, fold the spinach into the roasted vegetables and place back in the oven for 5 more minutes. Drizzle over the balsamic glaze and mix well. Serve on warm plates, with the carved duck on top of the roasted vegetables.

Slow Cooked Duck Legs with Red Wine and Mushroom Sauce

A great winter warmer, this lovely braised recipe has a rich savoury finish to complement the tasty meat. Delicious served with rice or mashed potatoes and steamed vegetables.

Serves: 2 | Preparation time: 30 minutes | Cooking time: 1 hour

Ingredients

2 Gressingham duck legs

Good rapeseed oil

1 small onion, peeled and diced

1 small carrot, peeled and diced

1 clove of garlic, peeled and diced

1 tbsp plain flour

250ml good red wine

450ml chicken stock (homemade or from bouillon)

1 sprig of fresh thyme

1 bay leaf

2 tbsp smoked bacon lardons

2 large mushrooms, quartered

Method

Preheat the oven to 180°c or 160°c fan. Dry the duck legs with kitchen roll and season all over. Seal and brown the legs on both sides in a hot oiled pan over a high heat. Remove and keep warm.

In a little more oil over a medium heat, fry the onion, carrot and garlic until soft. Keep stirring them so they don't burn. Add the flour and stir constantly for 1 minute.

Add the wine and simmer until reduced by half, then add the stock, thyme and bay leaf along with the duck legs, placed skin side down into the sauce.

Cover the pan with an ovenproof lid or tin foil then bake in the oven for 1 hour or until the meat is tender. Alternatively, transfer everything to a lidded casserole dish before placing in the oven.

Meanwhile, fry the bacon and mushrooms in a little oil over a medium heat until brown. Add to the pan in the oven 20 minutes before the duck finishes cooking. Remove from the oven, divide the duck legs and sauce between warm plates, then serve with your choice of accompaniments.

Orange and Chilli Poussin

The citrus and spice in this smart supper recipe is always popular. Serve it with either simple buttered vegetables or on top of an Asian slaw with steamed rice.

Serves: 4-6 | Preparation time: 15 minutes | Cooking time: 1 hour

Ingredients

3 whole poussins

Good rapeseed oil

2 tsp dried oregano

1 tsp dried thyme

1 tsp ground cumin

1 tbsp smoked paprika

Salt and black pepper

175ml sweet chilli sauce

1 orange, zested

Method

Preheat your oven to 190°c or 170°c fan. Lightly oil the skin of the poussins. Mix the herbs and spices together then rub them onto the skin and also inside the cavity. Season well with salt and pepper then place the poussins in a deep-sided roasting tray skin side up. Cook for 1 hour in the preheated oven, occasionally basting the birds with the juices in the tin.

Meanwhile, mix the sweet chilli sauce with the orange zest. When the poussins have cooked for 30 minutes, pour the zesty sweet chilli sauce all over the poussins and cook for a further 15 minutes. Baste again and return to the oven for another 5 minutes. Remove from the oven and allow to rest for 10 minutes in a warm place before serving.

Joint the poussins and arrange them on top of your chosen accompaniments.

By William Buchanan, Gressingham's managing director, and his wife Becky

Confit Duck Legs

This classic yet versatile duck dish is delicious any time of the year. Traditionally, it would be served with a rich red wine sauce, mashed potato or Puy lentils and braised red cabbage. You could also quite easily shred the duck off the bone for a tasty warm salad.

Serves: 4 | Preparation time: 1 hour 15 minutes, plus overnight marinating | Cooking time: 3 hours 30 minutes

Ingredients

6 tbsp coarse rock salt

Few sprigs of rosemary and thyme

1 bulb of garlic, cloves separated, skins on, flattened with a large knife

4 large Gressingham duck legs

1 tsp whole black peppercorns

2 bay leaves

1 orange, zested

1kg duck fat

Method

You will need to start the confit process at least one day ahead. Scatter one fifth of the salt, herbs and garlic in a deep tray or dish big enough to hold the duck legs. Place the legs skin side down in the dish and sprinkle the rest of the salt, herbs and garlic over the legs along with the peppercorns, bay leaves and orange zest. Cover and place in the fridge overnight.

When you are ready to cook, remove the duck legs from the fridge, scrape off the herbs and salt, rinse under cold water and dry well with kitchen roll.

Preheat the oven to 125°c or 105°c fan. Place a large ovenproof saucepan or casserole dish on a low heat and melt the duck fat. Carefully place the duck legs into the pan or dish, ensuring they are fully covered by the fat. Cover with a lid or foil and place into the oven. Cook for 2 hours 30 minutes to 3 hours until tender. Test if the meat is ready by piercing with a skewer; it should be soft and yielding. If not, return to the oven and test every 30 minutes.

When the duck legs are ready, remove the pan or dish from the oven and allow them to cool in the fat for 1 hour. Take the legs out of the fat and place them on a wire rack in a roasting tray, skin side up. If you wish to store them at this stage, you can put the legs into a container, cover with duck fat, put the lid on and refrigerate for up to a month. Otherwise, keep the fat for your next batch of confit.

To roast your confit legs, preheat your oven to 200°c or 180°c fan. Place them in the oven and roast for about 30 minutes until the duck is heated through and the skin is crispy. To help speed up the process of crisping the skin, you can place them under a hot grill for the last couple of minutes before serving.

Duck Burgers with Sweet Potato Wedges and Slaw

You can't beat a burger in the summer months. Try our delicious duck version
packed with mayo, lettuce and gherkins.

Serves: 2 | Preparation time: 30 minutes | Cooking time: 20 minutes

Ingredients

For the wedges

1 large sweet potato, cut into wedges
1 tbsp olive oil
1 tbsp honey
1 tbsp lemon juice

For the burgers

210g pack of Gressingham
Crispy Aromatic Shredded Duck
140g sausagemeat
1 tbsp hoisin sauce
(from the pack of shredded duck)
1 tbsp onion jam or onion marmalade

For the slaw

½ a red onion, finely sliced
1 carrot, peeled into long strips
using a potato peeler
1 courgette, peeled into long strips
using a potato peeler
1 tbsp olive oil
½ tbsp lemon juice
Salt and black pepper

To assemble

2 tbsp mayonnaise
1 cos lettuce
2 brioche buns
1 large gherkin, sliced

Method

For the wedges

Place the sweet potato wedges on a baking tray, drizzle with the olive oil
and cook in the oven at 180°c for 20 minutes. Meanwhile, make the burger
patties and slaw.

For the burgers

Mix the shredded duck, sausagemeat, hoisin sauce and onion jam together
in a bowl, then shape the mixture into two patties. Heat a griddle pan and
cook the burgers for 6 minutes on each side, then remove and leave them
to rest for 3 minutes.

For the slaw

Toss the sliced onion and vegetable strips together in a bowl with the olive
oil and lemon juice, then season with salt and pepper to taste.

To assemble

Remove the sweet potato wedges from the oven, drizzle them with the
honey and lemon juice then return them to the oven to cook for a further
5 minutes.

Assemble the burgers with a dollop of mayonnaise and two lettuce leaves
on the base of each bun, then the duck patties, then two or three slices of
gherkin. Top with the bun lids and serve with the crunchy slaw and sweet
potato wedges.

Duck Breast with Prunes and Carrots

Prunes might sound like an unusual match for duck, but their sweetness complements the rich flavour of the meat along with the carrots and honey.

Serves: 4 | Preparation time: 15 minutes | Cooking time: 30 minutes

Ingredients

2 medium-sized potatoes, peeled

4 Gressingham duck breasts

100ml double cream

1 tbsp unsalted butter, softened

6 medium carrots, peeled

2 tbsp runny honey

12 ready-to-eat soft dried prunes

Method

Preheat the oven to 180°c or 160°c fan. The potatoes, carrots and duck are cooked simultaneously so prepare everything first. Cut the peeled potatoes into large cubes and set aside. Cut the peeled carrots into thick batons.

Put the potatoes into a large pan of salted, boiling water then turn down the heat to a gentle simmer while you start the duck.

Dry the duck breasts well on kitchen paper. Lightly score the skin with a sharp knife six to eight times along the duck breast (to help the fat render out and flavour the meat). Season well with salt and pepper. Lay the duck breasts skin side down into a cold, unoiled, ovenproof frying pan.

Cook over a low-medium heat for about 6 to 8 minutes until the skin is golden and crispy, while regularly draining off any fat carefully into a bowl. Turn the duck breasts over to seal the meat side for 30 seconds and then transfer to the preheated oven. Roast for 10 to 20 minutes (depending on how well done you like your duck).

Once the potatoes are tender, drain well and place back into the saucepan over the turned-off hob to steam dry for a few minutes. Meanwhile, heat the cream with the butter until steaming. Mash the potatoes well or push them through a potato ricer. Stir the hot buttery cream into the potatoes and season to taste. Cover and keep warm.

Remove the duck breasts from the oven and rest somewhere warm for 5 minutes. Meanwhile, simmer the carrots in salted water for 5 to 10 minutes until tender.

Heat up the duck frying pan with a little of the reserved fat over a medium-high heat and fold in the carrots along with the honey. Gently fry, turning over the carrots occasionally until lightly caramelised. Fold through the prunes, turn off the heat and keep warm.

To serve, thinly carve the duck breasts and serve on a bed of mashed potato, surrounded by the honeyed carrots and prunes.

By James Jay, head chef at the Easton White Horse

Duck Jungle Curry

A great curry packed full of flavour and spice. We use half a roast aromatic duck here but you can use any leftover duck, or simply roast two duck legs then serve them whole on top of the curry or shred them into the sauce. Serve with steamed rice.

Serves: 2 | Preparation time: 30 minutes | Cooking time: 30 minutes

Ingredients

For the curry paste

1 lemongrass stalk

2cm root ginger, peeled and roughly chopped

2 small onions, peeled and roughly chopped

6 cloves of garlic, peeled

2 red chillies, roughly chopped

1 tbsp lemon juice

1 tbsp vegetable oil

1 tsp white pepper

½ tsp ground turmeric

For the curry

1 Gressingham half aromatic duck

2 tbsp vegetable oil

5 kaffir lime leaves

200g butternut squash

1 aubergine

200ml chicken stock

1 tin of coconut milk (400ml)

2 tbsp fish sauce

2 tsp palm sugar

Method

Preheat the oven to 200°c or 180°c fan. Remove any packaging from the half aromatic duck, place it on a baking tray and roast in the preheated oven for 30 minutes.

Meanwhile, make the curry paste. Remove the hard end and dry top half of the lemongrass stalk, then roughly chop the remainder. Grind all the ingredients for the paste together in a pestle and mortar. Alternatively, you could blitz everything in a blender to a smooth consistency.

Put a large pan onto a low-medium heat and pour in the oil, then add the curry paste and lime leaves. Cook for 10 minutes, stirring occasionally and adding a little water if anything starts to stick. Meanwhile, prepare the butternut squash and the aubergine by peeling the squash, topping and tailing the aubergine, then chopping both into 2cm dice.

Add the butternut squash and aubergine to the pan, lightly season and stir for 2 minutes. Pour in the stock and coconut milk, bring to the boil and then simmer until the duck has finished roasting. Remove the duck from the oven, carefully shred the meat off the bones with two forks and add it to the curry sauce along with the fish sauce and palm sugar. Stir everything together and simmer for a further 10 minutes, adding a touch of water if the sauce is drying out too much.

When the curry is almost ready, stir in the mangetout and adjust the seasoning after tasting the sauce. Spoon the curry into two warm bowls and garnish with fresh basil just before serving.

By Paul Thompson at Paul Thompson Events

Roast Squash Orzotto with Duck Breast

The same slow-cooked style of dish as risotto; when made with pearl barley, this Italian classic is called an orzotto. The rich duck provides a savoury, meaty accompaniment to the sweet squash.

Serves: 2 | Preparation time: 40 minutes | Cooking time: 30 minutes

Ingredients

2 Gressingham duck breasts

350g butternut squash, peeled and diced

2 tbsp olive oil

2 cloves of garlic, crushed

½ a red onion, sliced

125ml good dry white wine

1 chicken stock cube, dissolved in 500ml hot water

125g pearl barley, cooked in boiling water for 25 minutes then drained

50g butter

A few sage leaves, finely sliced

½ a red chilli, deseeded and finely sliced

Method

Preheat your oven to 180°c or 160°c fan. Dry the duck breasts well with kitchen roll. Lightly score the skin six to eight times with a sharp knife. Season on both sides.

Place the duck in a cold pan with no oil on a low to medium heat, and fry for about 6 minutes until the skin is crisp and golden. Carefully pour off any fat into a bowl as you cook. Transfer the duck breasts to the preheated oven for 6 to 8 minutes, longer if you prefer your duck well done. Remove and rest somewhere warm for 5 to 10 minutes.

Meanwhile, in another frying pan over a low to medium heat fry the butternut squash with the olive oil until it starts to soften. Stir in the garlic and onion then cook for a further 5 minutes.

Turn up the heat, pour in the wine and half the chicken stock, then bring to the boil. Fold in the pearl barley and cook until it takes on a risotto-like appearance and consistency. Add more liquid gradually if it's drying out too quickly. Stir in any juices from the resting duck.

In a small pan, quickly melt the butter then drop in the sage and chilli.

Season the orzotto to taste then serve in warm bowls. Carve the duck into thick slices, place on top of the orzotto and drizzle the sage and chilli butter over to finish.

SIMPLE
SAUCES

Honey and Soy Marinade

A quick and simple honey and soy marinade for duck. This recipe is especially good for the barbecue. Alternatively, use a hot griddle pan indoors.

Serves: 4-6 | Preparation time: 10 minutes

Ingredients

4 tbsp vegetable oil

5 tbsp runny honey

5 tbsp light soy sauce

½ tbsp ground black pepper

Method

Mix together all the ingredients in a bowl. Paint a thin layer of the marinade onto your whole duck, duck legs or duck breasts before cooking.

Cook your chosen cut of duck on a preheated barbecue or in a griddle pan on the hob. Towards the end of the cooking time, baste the meat with some more marinade and finish off grilling the duck until brown and caramelised.

Redcurrant Jus

This sauce is a deep and rich gravy, perfect for any cut of duck. For ease, it can be made in advance and reheated when you want to quickly rustle up a delicious meal.

Serves: 4 | Preparation time: 5 minutes | Cooking time: 15 minutes

Ingredients

200ml good red wine

1 tbsp good redcurrant jelly

1 tsp balsamic vinegar

500ml chicken stock (homemade or from bouillon)

A knob of butter

Method

Place the red wine, redcurrant jelly and balsamic vinegar into a small saucepan and reduce until the mixture starts to get sticky and dark.

Add the chicken stock and bring back to the boil to reduce the liquid by three quarters, down to a sauce consistency.

Whisk in the knob of butter and then take off the heat before seasoning to taste.

Red Wine Gravy

We show you how to make a luxurious, rich accompaniment to complement your meal. Perfect with any of our roasted birds for Sunday lunch.

Serves: 4 | Preparation time: 10 minutes | Cooking time: 10 minutes

Ingredients

1 pack of giblets (from the bird you are roasting)

1 onion, halved

1 large carrot, roughly chopped

1 stick of celery, roughly chopped

1 bay leaf

6 peppercorns

850ml boiling water

Knob of unsalted butter

1½ tbsp plain flour

375ml good red wine

1 tbsp redcurrant jelly (optional)

Method

First you need to make the stock, which can be done ahead of time. Wash the giblets and place them into a large saucepan. Add all the vegetables, bay leaf, peppercorns and boiling water. Bring back to the boil and then gently simmer for 1 hour. Carefully strain the stock through a sieve. Keep warm if using straight away or cool and refrigerate for later.

Make the gravy once your duck is cooked and you have strained off most of the fat (leaving a few tablespoons of fatty juices) from your hob proof roasting tin. Place the tray over a low to medium heat on the hob and add the butter. Let it melt then sprinkle in the flour and mix well with a whisk.

Once the tin is hot, pour in the wine and turn up the heat to high. Whisk well until it thickens. Then start slowly adding ladles of stock, whisking continually until it has all been mixed in.

Simmer over a low to medium heat and reduce until you have the consistency you prefer. Season to taste. If you prefer a sweeter gravy you can stir in a generous tablespoon of redcurrant jelly before serving with your roast duck.

Blackberry and Port Sauce

A deliciously rich, boozy sauce with the balancing sharp flavour of the berries. It works perfectly with well-seasoned whole birds or joints of duck.

Serves: 4 | Preparation time: 5 minutes | Cooking time: 35 minutes

Ingredients

350ml good Port

400ml chicken stock

1 small punnet of blackberries

1 tbsp balsamic vinegar

2 tsp caster sugar

1 star anise

1 tsp cornflour, mixed with a little water to make a slurry

50g butter

Method

Pour the Port into a hot saucepan and reduce over a high heat until you have about half the volume of liquid. This will take 10 to 15 minutes.

Stir in the stock, blackberries, vinegar, sugar and star anise. Bring to the boil and reduce again by two thirds, stirring occasionally to avoid sticking. This will take around 15 minutes.

Push the sauce through a sieve into another pan. Place on a medium heat, stir in the cornflour slurry, season and simmer for a few minutes until the mixture thickens. Stir in the butter and serve with your chosen cooked duck and favourite vegetables.

Cherry and Red Wine Sauce

A speedy addition to a sumptuous supper menu that can be made in advance
and heated up when needed.

Serves: 4 | Preparation time: 5 minutes | Cooking time: 15 minutes

Ingredients

50g caster sugar

3 tbsp red wine vinegar

175ml good red wine

400ml chicken stock (homemade or from bouillon)

12 pitted cherries (fresh or preserved)

1 tsp cherry or redcurrant jam (optional)

Method

Place the sugar and red wine vinegar in a saucepan on a medium heat and simmer until reduced to a sticky caramel.

Pour in the wine and stock to heat through and reduce again by two thirds. Stir in the cherries.

Season to taste and if the sauce requires more sweetness, stir in the jam.

Orange and Chilli Sauce For Duck

In just 10 minutes you can whip up a sweet and tangy orange sauce for duck with a spicy twist.

Serves: 2-3 | Preparation time: 5 minutes | Cooking time: 5 minutes

Ingredients

1 large orange, zested and juiced

150ml pineapple juice

½ a chilli, finely chopped

1 tbsp caster sugar

1 tsp cornflour

4 orange segments

Small handful of fresh coriander leaves

Method

Place the orange zest and juice, pineapple juice, chilli and sugar in a saucepan. Bring to the boil and reduce the amount of liquid by a third over a high heat.

Mix the cornflour with a little water to form a slurry then stir this into the sauce, turning the heat to low. Simmer and stir for a few minutes until the mixture thickens.

Fold the orange segments and fresh coriander into the sauce just before serving.

By Geoff Buchanan, Gressingham's managing director and his wife Ali

Perfect Plum Sauce

It's hard to believe that a recipe as simple and quick as this can taste so good with duck, but it's delicious! No fuss, no bother, just so tasty and the perfect partner for duck breasts.

Serves: 4 | Preparation time: 5 minutes | Cooking time: 15 minutes

Ingredients

400g fresh plums, destoned

125ml dry white wine

1 bay leaf, fresh is preferable

1 tbsp sherry vinegar

2-3 tbsp caster sugar, to taste

Method

Cook the plums, wine and bay leaf together in a lidded saucepan over a low to medium heat until the fruit totally collapses. Remove the bay leaf and process with a hand blender or a food processor until you have a smooth purée.

While the sauce is still warm, fold in the sherry vinegar and then start mixing in sugar to taste. You are looking for a good balance of tart and sweet flavour in the sauce. Season with salt and pepper to suit. Easy!

INDEX

Gressingham guinea fowl

Whole Roast Guinea Fowl with Roasted Root Vegetables 81

Roast Guinea Fowl 128

Gressingham half aromatic duck

Crispy Duck Salad with Hoisin Dressing 38

Duck Noodle Soup 50

Duck Jungle Curry 164

Gressingham stir fry strips

Duck Stir Fry with Oyster Sauce 52

Gressingham turkey

Festive Roast Turkey 132

H

harissa paste

Moroccan Duck Salad 78

hazelnuts

Roasted Duck Legs with Figs and Choucroute 84

hoisin sauce

Crispy Duck Salad with Hoisin Dressing 38

Crispy Aromatic Duck Pancakes 56

Hoisin and Soy Roasted Duck Platter 62

Duck Burgers with Sweet Potato Wedges and Slaw 160

honey

Roast Duck Breast and Walnut Salad 32

Duck and Pak Choi Noodles 61

Honey and Orange Glazed Duck Breast 72

Moroccan Duck Salad 78

Duck Breast with Cherries 82

Duck Paella 110

Middle Eastern Shredded Duck Wraps 116

Glazed Cardamom and Honey Whole Roast Duck 124

Whole Roast Duck with Honey and Rosemary 127

Roast Parsnips 139

Honey and Marmalade Duck Legs with Sweet Potato Mash 147

Duck Burgers with Sweet Potato Wedges and Slaw 160

Duck Breast with Prunes and Carrots 163

Honey and Soy Marinade 170

hummus

Middle Eastern Shredded Duck Wraps 116

K

kale

Roast Duck Legs with Blackberry and Port Sauce 90

kidney beans

Chilli con Canard 103

L

leek

Duck Croquettes 100

Puff Pastry Duck Pie 115

lemon

Moroccan Duck Salad 78

Duck Breast with Tomato and Basil Pasta 88

Zesty Roast Spatchcock Poussin 104

Middle Eastern Shredded Duck Wraps 116

Summer Roast Duck Crown 122

Apple Sauce 138

Vichy Carrots 139

Piri Piri Spatchcock Poussin and Cumin Potatoes 144

Duck Burgers with Sweet Potato Wedges and Slaw 160

Duck Jungle Curry 164

lime

Duck Filo Rolls with Sweet Chilli and Lime Mayo 30

Crispy Duck Salad with Hoisin Dressing 38

Five Spice Duck Leg and Asian Slaw 58

Thai Duck Salad with Lime, Chilli and Garlic Dressing 66

Chilli con Canard 103

Vietnamese Table Salad with Roast Poussin 109

Duck Jungle Curry 164

M

manchego

Duck Croquettes 100

mangetout

Duck Jungle Curry 164

mango chutney

Duck Filo Rolls with Sweet Chilli and Lime Mayo 30

marmalade

Honey and Marmalade Duck Legs with Sweet Potato Mash 147

mayonnaise

Duck Filo Rolls with Sweet Chilli and Lime Mayo 30

Duck Steak and Fries 35

Duck Croquettes 100

Zesty Roast Spatchcock Poussin 104

Summer Roast Duck Crown 122

Duck Burgers with Sweet Potato Wedges and Slaw 160

rice vermicelli noodles

Duck Noodle Soup 50

Vietnamese Table Salad with
Roast Poussin 109

Rioja

Duck Paella 110

roasted peanuts

Duck Panang Curry 87

rocket

Crispy Duck Salad with
Hoisin Dressing 38

Roasted Duck Legs with Figs
and Choucroute 84

Parmentier de Canard (Duck
'Shepherd's Pie') 112

S

salad leaves

Roast Duck Breast and
Walnut Salad 32

Crispy Duck Salad with
Hoisin Dressing 38

Five Spice Duck Leg and
Asian Slaw 58

Thai Duck Salad with Lime, Chilli
and Garlic Dressing 66

Pulled Duck and Sweet Chilli 75

sauerkraut

Roasted Duck Legs with Figs
and Choucroute 84

savoy cabbage

Duck Breast with Balsamic Dressing
and Cabbage 42

Country Duck Soup 98

Fried Pheasant Breast with
Pancetta and Sage 151

shallot

Duck Breast with Cherries 82

Roasted Duck Legs with Figs
and Choucroute 84

Roast Duck Legs with Blackberry and
Port Sauce 90

sherry

Crispy Aromatic Duck Pancakes 56

Hoisin and Soy Roasted
Duck Platter 62

Glazed Cardamom and Honey
Whole Roast Duck 124

sherry vinegar

Perfect Plum Sauce 176

shredded duck

Duck Filo Rolls with Sweet Chilli and
Lime Mayo 30

Crispy Duck Salad with
Hoisin Dressing 38

Duck Noodle Soup 50

Duck Panang Curry 87

Country Duck Soup 98

Duck Croquettes 100

Chilli con Canard 103

Middle Eastern Shredded
Duck Wraps 116

Slow Cooker Red Thai Duck and
Sweet Potato Curry 118

Duck Burgers with Sweet Potato
Wedges and Slaw 160

smoked bacon lardons

Canard au Vin 106

Slow Cooked Duck Legs with Red
Wine and Mushroom Sauce 154

smoked streaky bacon

Duck Breast with Balsamic Dressing
and Cabbage 42

Fried Pheasant Breast with Pancetta
and Sage 151

soured cream

Chilli con Canard 103

spaghetti

Duck Breast with Tomato and
Basil Pasta 88

spinach leaves

Roast Duck Breast with Balsamic
Glazed Root Vegetables 152

spring onions

Duck Filo Rolls with Sweet Chilli
and Lime Mayo 30

Crispy Duck Salad with
Hoisin Dressing 38

Duck à l'orange 45

Duck Noodle Soup 50

Duck Stir Fry with Oyster Sauce 52

Crispy Aromatic Duck Pancakes 56

Hoisin and Soy Roasted
Duck Platter 62

Twice Cooked Duck Stir Fry with
Black Bean Sauce 65

Pulled Duck and Sweet Chilli 75

Vietnamese Table Salad with
Roast Poussin 109

swede

Country Duck Soup 98

Roast Duck Breast with Balsamic
Glazed Root Vegetables 152

sweet chilli sauce

Duck Filo Rolls with Sweet Chilli
and Lime Mayo 30

Sticky Sweet Chilli Duck Legs 36

Pulled Duck and Sweet Chilli 75

Vietna124mese Table Salad with
Roast Poussin 109

Orange and Chilli Poussin 157

sweet peppers

Duck Paella 110

sweet potatoes

Duck Breast with
Sweet Potato Mash 46

Slow Cooker Red Thai Duck and
Sweet Potato Curry 118

Honey and Marmalade Duck Legs
with Sweet Potato Mash 147

Duck Burgers with Sweet Potato
Wedges and Slaw 160

szechuan peppercorns

Crispy Aromatic Duck Pancakes 56

T

tahini

Middle Eastern Shredded
Duck Wraps 116

tamarind purée

Tamarind and Ginger Duck Breast 55

tea leaves

Tea-Smoked Duck Breast Salad 148

Thai curry paste

Duck Panang Curry 87

Slow Cooker Red Thai Duck and
Sweet Potato Curry 118

tomato

Thai Duck Salad with Lime, Chilli
and Garlic Dressing 66

Duck Breast with Tomato and
Basil Pasta 88

Duck Cassoulet 93

Country Duck Soup 98

Chilli con Canard 103

Puff Pastry Duck Pie 115

Summer Roast Duck Crown 122

tomato purée

Country Duck Soup 98

Chilli con Canard 103

Puff Pastry Duck Pie 115

tortilla chips

Chilli con Canard 103

tortilla wraps

Middle Eastern Shredded
Duck Wraps 116

W

walnuts

Roast Duck Breast and
Walnut Salad 32

white cabbage

Crispy Duck Salad with
Hoisin Dressing 38

white wine

Roasted Duck Legs with Figs
and Choucroute 84

Duck Cassoulet 93

Zesty Roast Spatchcock Poussin 104

Whole Roast Duck with Honey
and Rosemary 127

Roast Squash Orzotto with
Duck Breast 167

Perfect Plum Sauce 176

white wine vinegar

Roast Duck Breast and
Walnut Salad 32

Piri Piri Spatchcock Poussin and
Cumin Potatoes 144

whole Gressingham duck

Hoisin and Soy Roasted
Duck Platter 62

Glazed Cardamom and Honey
Whole Roast Duck 124

Whole Roast Duck with Honey
and Rosemary 127

Y

yellow pepper

Five Spice Duck Leg and
Asian Slaw 58

Twice Cooked Duck Stir Fry with
Black Bean Sauce 65

yoghurt

Middle Eastern Shredded
Duck Wraps 116